LAND FIT FOR HEROES

Marie Keates

During the General Strike of 1926, an unpaid debt and an unsolved murder tests the friendship between two Southampton dockers, and uncovering the truth becomes a matter of life and death.

Percy sees the strike as a chance to recapture the dreams snatched away from him on a battlefield in France. Meanwhile, Lenny is tired of constantly bailing out his brother-in-law, but he can't forget what Percy sacrificed for him. Laura is caught between the two men she loves. She's exasperated by her brother Percy's self-destructive behaviour and worried about the toll it's taking on her husband, Lenny.

Then Percy gets involved with a criminal gang. When the violence starts to escalate, he turns detective after suspecting they may be behind a shocking unsolved crime. Has he bitten off more than he can chew? And will his digging drag Lenny down with him? If it does, what will become of Laura and her children?

For Leonard Arthur White

1 - Saturday 24 April 1926

When Lenny saw young Albie Joyce on the doorstep, he knew he was in for a long night. He liked Albie; he was a good lad and a hard worker, but there was only one reason he'd be knocking on the door at nine o'clock on a Saturday evening.

'It's Percy.' Albie was a little out of breath. His collar was turned up and rainwater dripped from his cap.

'Isn't it always,' Lenny sighed. He looked over Albie's shoulder at the teeming rain. The house lights and streetlights reflected gold in the growing puddles, and chilly air, thick with the acrid smell of the gasworks, drifted into the hallway. 'What's he done now?'

'He's got in a brawl with some posh chap in the Bell and Crown.' Albie took his cap off, shook off the water and nervously smoothed back his thick, dark hair. 'It wasn't his fault this time. The chap was with a load of fascists. They were calling us all Bolsheviks and boasting how a strike might be coming but they would break it. Then one of them started on Percy. I think he saw his scar and knew he'd been in the war. Anyway, he started spouting all this stuff about the Tommies who joined the strike being traitors to their country, and how being a communist and downing tools was like tramping on the graves of the brave men who died in France. Percy went mad. If Harry Smith, Arthur Fisk and Jimmy Pothecary hadn't been there, who knows what might have happened? The other fascists all scarpered.'

'Is he still at the pub?'

'He was when I left. Harry told me to come and get you.'

With an exasperated huff, Lenny went to get his coat and tell Laura where he was going. The steady drip of water falling into the bucket on the upstairs landing reminded him that the hole in the roof was getting bigger. He'd had a hard day at work. He was tired. The last thing he wanted to do was go out into the rain and cold, but there was no way round it. Worrying about Percy and bailing him out of trouble came as naturally as breathing. He'd been doing it now for almost ten years.

'Not again.' Laura looked up from her sewing and shook her head when he told her what had happened. 'That bloody brother of mine is more trouble than he's worth. I swear I'm going to swing for him one of these days.'

Lenny loved how she never minced her words almost as much as he loved her plump prettiness, her eyes like dark chocolate drenched with honey and her quick smile. On the outside she was so soft and curvaceous, but she was as hard as diamond on the inside.

'I'll try to bring him back in one piece. Don't wait up, though.' He picked up his coat and hat and pecked her on the cheek.

The Bell and Crown was only at the end of the road. With any luck Percy would still be there, and he wouldn't be so drunk he'd need Albie to help carry him back.

'Was there much damage?' Lenny asked as they marched up the road, heads down against the rain.

'Not as far as I could see. Maybe a few broken glasses and some chairs turned over. Percy didn't have a mark on him, either. The bloke barely had a chance to get a punch in.'

'Sounds about right.'

When it came to fighting, Percy waded in as if he were immortal, but he never seemed to get injured. It was almost as if he'd used up all his bad luck over in France.

Although the pub was no more than three-hundred yards away, Lenny was soaked through by the time he pushed the door open. The place was packed to the rafters, mostly with dockers celebrating the end of another working week. The air was thick with smoke and the smell of damp, sweaty bodies. Someone was playing *Don't Dilly Dally* on the piano, although Lenny couldn't actually see them through the crowd. A few people joined in with the chorus.

'You can't trust a "Special"

Like the old-time copper

When you can't find your way home.'

He wasn't much of a drinker, but he'd dragged Percy out of this pub enough times to know it well. He shouldered his way through the crowd. As he went, he looked around for Percy, or any sign there'd been a fight. He found neither, but he did find Amy Medway, the landlady, pulling pints at the bar.

'For once it wasn't his fault,' she said, giving him a wry smile.

With her shock of molasses-brown curls and meaty arms any docker would envy, it was hard to tell her age. He'd have put her somewhere between forty and fifty, but she could easily be far younger or far older.

'Is he still here?' He looked up and down the bar, as if Percy might suddenly materialise.

'No. Harry Smith and Jimmy Pothecary took the toff off somewhere, and I told Arthur Fisk to take Percy off, too, in case the coppers turned up looking for him. Broke one of me chairs, they did, and half a dozen glasses, but Harry Smith took a couple of quid out of the toff's wallet to pay for it all. He had more than a fiver in there, believe it or not. What's a rich chap like that doing round here anyway? Harry told me, "If anyone comes asking about this, it never happened." So, I says, "I'll tell 'em these chaps came in and started busting the place up for no reason, and me regulars threw 'em out on the street." They'll all vouch for it, and they'll swear Percy was never here tonight.'

'Do you know where Percy and Arthur were heading?'

'No, but I know Arthur lives in Chapel Road. He sometimes drinks in the Apollo, and the Durham.'

He thanked Amy and pushed his way back out into the rain, with Albie trailing behind him like a lost puppy. With his head down against the icy air he splashed his way towards Chapel Road. It wasn't a long walk, but the streets were sloshing with water. It always flooded here when it rained heavily. To add to his misery, now his feet were wet. Without the benefit of alcohol to dull his senses, he was cold, weary and more than a little angry at being dragged out of his warm house. How many times would he have to bail Percy out before his debt to him was repaid? If not for Laura, the bond between them might have been broken by now. Then again, who was he kidding? If he lived to be a hundred, he'd be beholden to Percy for what he'd done for him in France. He'd never get over the guilt of walking away unharmed from the shell that ruined Percy's life. If Percy had been paying more attention out there, instead of being intent on looking after him, he might not have been hit at all.

Finally, they reached the Apollo, but there was no sign of Percy. He wasn't in the Durham Tavern either, but Dan Painter said, 'If he's with Arthur Fisk I'd try the Royal Albert on Albert Road. He's got his eye on the barmaid in there; not that she'd look twice at a chancer like him.'

With a pub on every street corner and Percy's habit of drinking in all of them until he got thrown out or barred, it looked like it was going to be a long, wet night. Lenny and Albie made their way through the sodden streets towards Albert Road. It was anyone's guess whether they'd have any more luck there.

'You and Percy were in the army together in France, weren't you?' Albie asked as they walked.

'We were.'

The lad was not yet twenty, with a string bean body that looked as if it was trying hard to grow into his head. He was too young to have gone to France. Lenny looked at his fresh face and innocent, hazel eyes and found it hard to believe that at a similar age he'd been shovelling up rotting bodies in No Man's Land.

'What was it like?'

'Hell on earth.'

Hieronymus Bosch sprang to mind, but the reference would have been as lost on Albie as it would have been on everyone Lenny knew. Not even Laura understood his love of art. It was hardly a normal interest for a docker.

'Is that why Percy's like he is? He was badly wounded, wasn't he?'

'He almost lost his leg. A man is never the same after a thing like that.'

Despite the rain, men spilled out onto the street outside the Royal Albert. They all looked crumpled and grubby, as if they'd hit the pub straight from the dock gate. They most likely had, and they were now too full of drink to care about getting wet. They pushed their way into the pub. Lenny spotted Percy at once. There was no mistaking that tall, muscular physique, the mop of shaggy hair the colour of roasted coffee beans or the face that might have been handsome without the puckered scar running down his right cheek from the corner of his eye to his mouth. He stood at the bar with Arthur Fisk. Percy's height and Arthur's dark, cheeky cockiness made them an intimidating pair. If the toff at the Bell and Crown was itching for a fight he couldn't have picked on a worse target.

'You're for it now, Percy.' Arthur leaned back against the bar and wiped beer froth from his thin moustache with the back of his hand. His round, cherubically chubby face and wide blue eyes gave him a look of innocence belied by his sneering mouth and quick fists. 'Your sister's sent the cavalry out to fetch you home.'

Lenny curled his lip. He didn't much care for Arthur. He was too full of himself by far.

'If our Lor wanted me fetched she'd come herself, and she'd make mincemeat out of a young whippersnapper like you, Arthur, so less of your cheek.' Percy turned and grinned at Lenny. 'If it ain't my old pal Lofty come to join me for a pint before last orders.'

'I'd rather just go home.'

The use of his old army nickname told Lenny that Percy had had more than enough to drink already, although he was still standing, so he'd probably be able to get him back home on his own.

'Oh, come on. Just one for the road.' Percy pulled a handful of coins from his pocket and slapped them down onto the bar. 'And one for young Albie, too – for his trouble.'

Lenny knew this was a battle he couldn't win. He'd been down this road too many times before.

'Just one,' he nodded.

As he did so, he caught sight of his reflection in the mirror behind the bar; a pale, gaunt face and a shock of damp, blonde hair, half a head taller than everyone around him. He looked worse than he felt, and that was saying something.

2 - Sunday 25 April 1926

The scrawny chicken was in the oven and the smell of it roasting already permeated the dingy little kitchen. Frankly, it looked more pigeon than chicken, but it was all they could afford seeing as Percy had barely had a shift last week. Laura stood at the big white sink peeling potatoes with more viciousness than was strictly necessary. She was angry with Percy. Fuming, actually. It wasn't just about him pissing so much money up the wall and getting into brawls, it was all the time she wasted worrying about him, and the toll it took on Lenny. He'd made a fool of them yet again, and he didn't seem the least bit contrite about it. When he came into the kitchen, she couldn't even bring herself to turn to look at him.

'Shall I put the kettle on and make some tea?' He sounded sheepish as he put the battered old kettle on the range. 'Len will probably be getting up in a minute, I should think. Unless he's planning on sleeping all day.'

'Do what you bloody well like.' She turned to face him. The knife was still in her hand and she waved it in his direction. 'You always do anyway, and don't you dare malign Lenny. He got soaked to the skin chasing around after you last night. He was up half the night coughing. You know full well how bad he gets. He should never have had to go out in that weather.'

'Oh, don't be like that, Lor.' He tilted his head to one side and gave her a dejected smile. 'It was just a few drinks with the lads from the docks and a stupid toff who didn't know when to keep his mouth shut. He started it, not me. There was no need for Len to come out. Harry Smith had it all under control.'

'No bloody need.' If he thought his little boy lost look was going to wash with her now he was sadly mistaken. It might have worked when they were kids but he was a man now, with a stubbly chin and a neck as thick as his head. She had a sudden vision of plunging the knife into him. In case she was tempted to actually do it, she put it down. 'I'd say there was every bloody need. Albie reckoned you'd have killed that chap if Harry Smith and his mates hadn't stopped you.'

'I didn't start the fight. Ask Amy Medway, she'll tell you.'

'Of course she will, you're her best bloody customer. Anyway, I don't know why you're hanging around with that lot in the first place. They're nothing but a load of bloody Bolsheviks. What were you thinking going from pub to pub getting drunk with a load of communist dockers, plotting revolutions and strikes and god only knows what else?'

'It was just talk, a bit of solidarity with the miners. The mine owners are going to lock them out at the end of the month if they don't agree to a pay cut and longer hours. Working class men have to stand together.'

'Stand together until it all goes wrong. Then who do you

think they'll point the finger of blame at, eh? You've got scapegoat written all over your face, Percy Barfoot.'

'You're making a mountain out of a molehill. It was just talk, Lor.'

'A molehill, is it? Were you planning on starting the revolution last night before you got drunk and began picking fights with strangers? Was it all going to be war on the streets and dragging the rich men out of their beds to execute them, just like the Russians did to their Tsar and his whole family? Or maybe you were going to build a guillotine like the bloody French? Only, if that's the plan, you should let me know. I could bring my knitting and come along to watch. I'd far rather that than have poor Lenny running around in the cold and rain looking for you.'

'He didn't need to come looking for me.'

He couldn't even meet her eyes. Instead, he found something extremely interesting in the bottom corner of the scuffed and chipped kitchen cabinet. He wouldn't find any answers in the layers of peeling paint, no matter how long he looked.

'Didn't he? Should he have waited until you got arrested for treason, or you were swinging from the bloody gallows before he came after you? You'd have probably spent the night lying in the gutter if he hadn't, or in the police cells. He was soaked through and frozen half to death when he got in. Not that you give a flying fig about that. You're the only one who's allowed to suffer in this family,

17

aren't you? I doubt you even remember that Lenny was gassed. Only your war wounds count.'

Her eyes flicked to the scar running down his cheek. This was no time for pity, though. Just because Lenny's wounds weren't visible didn't make them any the less.

'That's not fair, Lor.' He caught her eye briefly then looked away again.

'I'll tell you what's not fair, Percy.' She stepped towards him and jabbed at his chest with her finger. 'Taking advantage of Lenny's kindness. Spending all your money in the pub instead of paying your keep. Letting him clear up all the trouble you make when you're drunk. Acting like you're the only man in England who got injured in the war. Wasting your whole life because things didn't go the way you wanted ten years ago. Most of all, it's not fair that every time you go out of that door, we should all have to worry what you're going to do next. It's time you bloody well grew up before you lose everyone in your life who actually cares about you.'

'I'm sorry.' He caught hold of her hand and didn't avoid her gaze this time.

'Well then, do something about it.' His eyes, chocolate brown and almond shaped, were so much like hers it was like looking in a mirror. There was remorse in them, but she'd seen that look too many times before to take it at face value. 'It's got to stop, Percy. I don't have the energy for it anymore, and neither does Lenny.'

3 - The Somme - November 1916

The ground was as hard as iron and little flakes of fine snow swirled around them as they stumbled over the shell-pocked earth searching for the dead. Some of the poor buggers had been lying out there in No Man's Land since the first day of the Somme Offensive; four months or more rotting in the mud. Finding the bodies amongst all the frozen mud and shell holes proved harder than Lenny had expected. When they came upon the first one, it was by accident. The Hun knew they were out there and what they were doing, and it wasn't long before they sent the first of the whizz-bangs over. He threw himself flat on his stomach, trembling. The ground beneath him was wet, stinking and slimy. He'd landed on a corpse, and not a fresh one, either. To his everlasting shame, he vomited.

'It's all right, mate.' Percy helped him to his feet. 'Happens to the best of us, but you soon get used to it.'

They managed to haul what was left of the poor blighter onto the stretcher by grabbing the sleeves of his jacket and the legs of his trousers. The stink was overpowering and Lenny couldn't stop retching. He couldn't believe he'd ever be able to take it in his stride like Percy.

Several bodies later, some transferred to the stretcher with the help of shovels, others nothing but skeletons in uniform, he'd stopped vomiting. He hadn't stopped seeing himself in every one of the poor sods, though. Would he end up this way, a white skull with a few tufts of blonde hair? Who would be shovelling what was left of him onto a stretcher? Every so often, another whizz-bang exploded. He got used to them surprisingly quickly. It wasn't as if he hadn't heard a shell explode before. He was just more used to hearing them from the other side of a trench. He knew this gave him a false sense of security, though, and that he could just as easily be killed there as out in the open.

Then Percy got hit. He didn't see it happen. He'd been kneeling over the corpse of Billy Simms. At least, it looked like it might have been Billy Simms once, before his flesh had been washed with a mixture of chrome green, Prussian blue and crimson. It wasn't a picture he wanted to paint, but he couldn't help thinking of it in those terms. The blast knocked him over and when he looked around, Percy was flat on the ground with an ashen face and blood pouring out of him. It was the shrapnel from the shell that had hit him, rather than the shell itself, so he was still alive, but he looked in a bad way. A flap of skin hung down from the side of his face, his arm was bleeding and the bone of his thigh stuck out through a bloody rip in his trousers. Lenny's stomach clenched at the sight, even though there was nothing left in it now. He couldn't understand how he'd been untouched.

'We need to get you back, mate,' he said, and looked at the ten yards or so between them and the trench. 'Maybe I should get some help?'

Percy had taken him under his wing when he first arrived, so now it was his turn to look after Percy.

'No,' Percy said through gritted teeth. 'I think I can walk if you help me, Lofty.'

This proved to be a touch over-optimistic, especially with him being so much taller and thinner than Percy. Somehow, though, he managed to get him upright and more or less carried him back to the trench. When they finally dropped breathlessly down to safety, they found Corporal Brodrick and Joe Wilson, all mud and tin helmets, crouched over the bodies they'd brought back. Joe tended Percy's wounds while Corporal Brodrick checked Lenny over to make sure he hadn't been hit, too. Luckily, he'd escaped with nothing but a few scrapes and grazes, but Percy was a different matter. His face and arm looked a lot worse than they were, but the leg was a mess. With a grim look, Joe bandaged it as best he could.

'Will I get three wound stripes or just one?' Percy could hardly speak for shivering, but it was likely shock rather than the cold. His skin had a bluish tinge and there were beads of sweat on his upper lip.

'Just the one, I think,' Joe said.

'How long before I'm back in action, do you reckon?'

'It'll be Blighty for you, mate,' Joe said. 'I'd say your war is probably over.'

When Percy began to cry, Lenny looked away, embarrassed to witness his friend's tears.

4 - Sunday 25 April 1926

Lenny was bone weary. He'd been awake half the night coughing. The more he fought it the worse it got. His chest bubbled and hissed like a cauldron and great barking fits exploded out of him. He knew he was keeping poor Laura awake and probably the children, too, but there was nothing he could do about it. It was the gas. It had ruined his lungs, and a night wandering around in the cold and wet had set it off again. The few hours' sleep he'd managed to snatch had been restless and filled with images of Percy's wounds.

Dragging him back home last night had reminded him so vividly of that journey across No Man's Land, except this time he carried Percy's weight because booze had stopped his legs working rather than a shell. They'd stumbled through the darkness, splashing through puddles shimmering chrome yellow with reflected streetlights and passing corner pubs where music and voices spilled out into the night. The rain beat down and gutters overflowed in cascading fountains. Percy sang *Take Me Back To Dear Old Blighty* and called him Lofty as if they were still in France.

Now he found Percy in the parlour, staring into the grate. Laura had laid the fire but it was too early in the day to light it. If there was any justice in the world, Percy would have a raging hangover, but for all his drinking he never suffered with them. Perhaps if he did, he'd drink less. Laura was in the kitchen cooking the dinner. It was the smell of the roasting chicken that had dragged him out of bed. Bobby and Gladys were out somewhere, probably trying to get a few lumps of coal or coke from the gasworks. He smiled at the memory of doing the same with his little brother, Jesse, when they lived around the corner in Standford Street. Mum would go mad at their filthy hands and faces, but she used what they found all the same. Then Jesse died. Mum said it was all the coal dust in the air and the mould on the walls. He must have been about Gladys's age, but he could still see Mum crying and Jesse lying still and pale in his little white coffin.

He sank onto the threadbare cushions of the battered wooden armchair opposite Percy. The day was dismal but neither had turned on the light; electricity was too expensive to waste needlessly. At least the gloom hid the peeling wallpaper and the general shabbiness of the room, even if it did nothing to disguise the smell of damp. After Jesse died, Lenny's poor old dad had worked himself half to death to get his family away from the gasworks. It gave Lenny hope that he might do the same some day, hopefully before he lost either of his children to the filthy air and the squalor. Lenny had been in France when his dad died. Afterwards, the family had scattered to the four winds, as if he'd been the glue holding them all together. Maybe that was why Laura's family meant so much to him.

'Laura's mad as hell with me.' Percy looked up from the piled coals.

'I gathered that.'

'It really wasn't my fault this time, though. That bloke just started on me for no reason. Harry thinks he was trying to provoke trouble and stir up some bad publicity for the strike.'

'It's not even certain there's going to be a strike yet, so why would he do that?'

'Harry says it's a foregone conclusion. The unions are determined to show solidarity with the miners, and rightly so. If we let the mine owners get away with cutting their money and increasing their hours, it's only a matter of time before the railway companies do the same, and they own the docks. A general strike is the only way to show them. He said that fascist toff knew he'd get a rise out of me by disrespecting the Tommies like that.' He looked down at his red, swollen knuckles. 'I probably shouldn't have taken the bait, but I'd had a few.'

'And therein lies the problem.' Lenny rubbed at his temples. Would Percy ever learn that drowning his troubles in booze only multiplied them? 'I wonder what Harry Smith did with the chap when he took him off.'

'He said he was going to dump him outside the police station. They poured a pint of beer over him so he'd smell like he was drunk. Waste of good beer in my opinion, but still . . .'

'You can't keep doing this, Percy. One of these days, you're going to go too far and end up swinging from a rope. Albie said it could have happened last night if Harry and the others hadn't been there.'

'I know.' Percy stared forlornly at his knuckles. 'Sometimes I think it would have been better if that shell had blown me to pieces, instead of just blowing bits of me to pieces.'

'That's just daft talk.'

It wasn't the first time Percy had said this kind of thing, but it didn't make it any easier to hear.

'Is it? You'd all be better off without me. All I do is cause trouble and upset everyone. You should've left me out there to bleed to death.'

'I don't think your mum and dad would agree with that, or Laura. Think about all the poor sods that didn't make it home. We are the lucky ones, mate.'

'I'm not so sure about that. Everything turned to rat shit when I got hit. All I ever wanted was to be a soldier. You wouldn't think it'd be too much to ask, would you? I joined the territorial force in September '13, the day after my seventeenth birthday. I wanted a proper career, not like Dad, who spent all his life labouring. I was going to really be something, win medals for gallantry, be a corporal, maybe a sergeant – or even better. Look at our Ethel's Ernie. He was a corporal at just twenty-two. That could have been me. I could have been an officer by now.' Percy paused and stared into the grate again, as if the answers to his problems lay there.

'It didn't get Ernie very far, did it? Unless you think riding round all day on the motor buses selling tickets is a good career.'

'Yes, that was what I wanted.' Percy carried on as if Lenny hadn't spoken. 'And I'd have got there too, if it hadn't been for that damned shell. Corporal Brodrick said I was going places. I didn't think it would be back to Blighty with a fucked-up leg, though. "Oh, you're so lucky," they all said, "you got a Blighty wound, you're out of it now." Well, I didn't want to be out of it. I didn't want to go home.'

'I know, mate, but you have to make the best of it. It was the luck of the draw. It could have been me just as easily.' The dim light hid Percy's scars, but the memory of how he got them haunted Lenny. A decade on and it was still so vivid it made him shudder just to think about it. Was it any wonder Percy couldn't forget, either? 'You can't waste the rest of your life feeling sorry for yourself. It's time to let it go before it destroys you.'

5 - Thursday 29 April 1926

Visiting Mum always made Laura feel oddly melancholic, even without the need to defend Percy. Something about being a guest in the house she once knew as home didn't feel right. Everything had changed but nothing had changed; the back parlour still had the same rose patterned wallpaper, the fireplace, the bevelled mirror hanging above it and the cups Dad had won for his vegetables remained on display atop the piano. Upstairs, the bedroom she'd once shared with Maria and Ethel was probably unchanged, too. Every room and every piece of furniture held a memory, but she was no longer part of it. Now her life was in the run-down terrace two miles away. Wherever she lived, though, she'd always end up as a buffer between her family and Percy.

'So, what's this I hear about our Percy taking up with the Bolsheviks?' Mum looked up from her knitting. Her long hair, twisted into a chignon at the nape of her neck, was more white than brown these days. She still wore corsets and blouses tucked into long fitted skirts, but her once trim waist had thickened and her large bust sagged. She was getting old, but at least Laura didn't have to worry so much about her and Dad now that her sister Maria was back home.

'Bad news travels fast, I see,' Laura muttered.

'Is it true, though?' Maria was only forty-three, but she looked old, too. She'd cut her chestnut-coloured hair short as a concession to the modern age, but it was sprinkled with grey and there were wrinkles around her eyes and deep furrows across her brow. She was knitting, too; a red jumper for her son, Stanley, by the look of it. She spoiled him, but that was understandable. He was her only child, and since last April, when Fred died, she'd clung to him as if her life depended on it. The poor lad had a permanently bewildered look on his face. He'd lost his father and was suffocated by his overprotective mother. You'd never have guessed he was the same age as Gladys. It wasn't only because he was so much smaller; there was also an air of fearfulness about him. Laura swore he was afraid of his own shadow. After what happened to Fred it was to be expected, but a boy of nearly six should be climbing trees and getting into mischief, not clinging to his mother's skirts. She'd said as much to Mum, but since Maria and Stanley had moved back into the family home, she'd been just as bad with the mollycoddling.

'Yes, it's true.' There was no point trying to hide it. They'd find out the details with or without her. 'He's got in with Harry Smith and his cronies. They've filled his head full of revolution and workers' rights.'

'Well, communism worked out well for the Russians, didn't it?' Mum placed her knitting on her lap and shook her head sadly. 'Six years of civil war and peasants starving, while the ones in charge sat in the old palaces and ate caviar. When is that boy going to grow up and start using his loaf? What is it with the men in this family? Seems to me only us women have any sense. The men are all brawn and no brain.'

'That's a bit unfair on Willy and Dad.' Laura didn't like the way this conversation was going.

'Is it?' Mum raised an eyebrow. 'All your dad cares about are plants and seeds, and William's still playing with bloody trains.'

'I'd hardly call being a shunter playing with trains, and they've both been good providers for their families,' Laura said. 'Kept nice roofs over their heads and food on the table.'

'If it weren't for me, and for William's Beatrice, I doubt there'd be either houses or food,' Mum sniffed. 'We're the ones who manage the money and organise everything. Without us they'd barely know when to get out of bed in the mornings, or have a table to put the food on. That's Percy's trouble. He hasn't got a woman to keep him on the straight and narrow. He's just bloody feckless. He needs someone to tell him what to do all the time, or he'll spend his life in the pub getting into bother.'

'Do you really think there will be more strikes?' Maria unrolled a tape measure and held it against her knitting. It looked like a sleeve, or maybe the front of a cardigan.

'Probably. It's all the dockers have been talking about,' Laura said. 'It's all "not a penny off the pay, not a minute on the day" at the dock gate. Anyone would think they were miners not dockers, but Percy says the docks will be next if the mine owners get away with it.'

'They're so stupid they can't grasp that they'll lose more money from a strike or a lock out than they ever would from the pay cut.' Mum shook her head sadly. 'All their talk about Triple Alliances and national strikes came to nought in '21. Lloyd George fooled them with his hogwash about public ownership and better conditions. Thirteen weeks the miners were out, and for what? And last year they thought Red Friday was a huge success. You mark my words, Baldwin's subsidy to the mine owners has all been a ruse to buy time. I'll wager they've set up all sorts of things to keep the coal coming and the country running. There's more than a million unemployed just waiting to take their jobs, strike or no strike, and cheap coal to import from America.'

'You don't have to convince me, Mum,' Laura said. 'I'm just worried about the dockers coming out on strike. I'm not sure I could stand weeks and weeks of it again. Last time, I thought we were going to starve or end up on the streets. It's all Percy talks about, though. Solidarity of the working classes and fighting for the 'land fit for heroes' they were promised after the war. He says any working-class man who doesn't vote for the Communist Party is a traitor or an idiot.'

'Well, he'd know all about idiots, that's for sure,' Mum laughed. 'Your father's the same, except he says vote Labour. Don't you dare tell him, but I voted for Baldwin last time.'

'So did I,' Maria whispered.

'If I'd been old enough to vote, I might have, too,' Laura said. 'Ramsay MacDonald might have been born working class, but I don't trust him, not after he denounced the treaty of Versailles and wanted to lend money to the Bolsheviks.'

'If only women ran the country,' Mum smiled.

6 - Saturday 1 May 1926

Percy burst into the kitchen whistling a merry tune and grinning. He passed Bobby and Gladys, who were shovelling down breakfast at the table, and peered through the grimy window into the backyard, as the first train of the day rattled the glass. Laura looked up from her sewing and smiled back.

'Looks like a nice day out there.' He kissed her on the cheek then turned to tickle Gladys under the chin. 'Make sure you wash behind those ears this morning. I think I can see some carrots and potatoes growing there.' Gladys giggled, pulled up her shoulders and tucked in her chin. Waves of hair, like burnt caramel, fell across her face. He reached behind her ear. 'What's this?' he said, holding up a silver sixpence.

Gladys gasped when he put it on the table in front of her. She put her hand to her ear, as if to check there was no more money hidden there. Bobby's eyes almost popped out of their sockets. Percy turned to him with a chuckle, tousled his white-blonde hair and said, 'Let's see what's growing behind your ears, young man.' Then he produced another sixpence and put it in his hand.

'You shouldn't spoil them, Percy. That's far too much.' Laura gave him an exasperated look and then glanced towards the hall, where Lenny was tapping his foot impatiently. 'Gladys, Bobby, what do you say?'

'Thank you, Uncle Percy,' they said in unison.

'Don't spend it all in one place.' He ruffled their hair.

'Come on, Percy, we'll be late,' Lenny called.

After the men had gone to work, Laura sat in the old chair by the range, stitched tiny, jet-black beads onto the hem of Hetty Porter's dress and watched Gladys and Bobby shovelling down their porridge at the table. They were both eager to finish their breakfast and get out to spend their money.

'Shall we get some sweets before we go to the picture house, Bobby?' Gladys swung her bare legs back and forth under the table.

She was her father's daughter for sure. All long, thin legs and arms, and the height of most eight-year-olds, even though she wasn't yet six. She had Laura's bubbly, outgoing temperament, but the only physical similarity was her hair and freckles.

'Not too many sweets,' Laura warned. 'You'll make yourselves sick. Don't spend all that money today, either. Or, if you do, don't come complaining to me when you don't have any left.'

'We can just ask Uncle Percy to look behind our ears again.' Bobby was deadly serious.

He was a year older than his sister and much quieter, more thoughtful and, like his father, slightly shy. His hair was a few shades lighter than Lenny's, but he had Laura's features and, like her, a tendency towards chubbiness, too.

'Good luck with that,' Laura laughed. 'I'll have to ask him to look behind my ears to see if he can find the money for the rent.'

*

By the time Gladys and Bobby left for the picture house with a crowd of other local children, Laura had finished Mrs Porter's dress. Percy hadn't come back, so he must have got a morning shift at least. If he was more reliable and less of a hothead he might get picked more often, but he was his own worst enemy. At least Lenny, with his beautiful handwriting, eye for detail and head for figures, was guaranteed regular work as a clerk. Instead of lumping around cargo like Percy, he checked and kept records of everything unloaded from the ships. If Percy was going to keep giving the children sixpences, he'd have to buck his ideas up, or maybe find a job elsewhere.

It was only a five-minute walk to Hetty Porter's house. It was a terrace like theirs but much nicer. For a start, it didn't look out over the gasworks. The same railway line ran at the bottom of Hetty's garden, but the air wasn't thick with the sulphurous stench of coal burned to create gas. She could open her windows and hang her washing on the line without the fear it would come in covered in soot and dirtier than it was before being washed. It had a bay window and a front garden rather than a door that opened straight onto the street, and inside it was all fresh paint and wallpaper, decent furniture and pretty knickknacks. It smelled of polish instead of damp, and the windows didn't rattle when a train went past.

'It's perfect!' Hetty turned this way and that in front of the full-length mirror in her bedroom. The dress, a simple shift cut in a slightly A-line shape to accommodate Hetty's small bust and wide hips, fit perfectly. The chocolate-coloured silk almost matched her hair, and the black beads at the hem caught the light beautifully. 'You really are very clever. Now, are you sure I don't owe you any extra? Those beads must have taken forever to sew on.'

'Nothing extra at all. I quoted you the full price right at the start, and I'd never think of asking for a penny more.'

'In that case, how about some pinafores for my daughter, like the ones you made for Rose? Two should be enough for now. I'm sure the extra money won't go amiss, especially with a strike imminent.'

'The unions are still negotiating, so I'm not sure it's imminent, but I'm happy to make you a couple of pinafores if you really need them.' Much as she wanted the money, she didn't want charity.

'You know what my Maisie's like. If she's not growing out of her clothes, she's ruining them somehow or losing them. She should have been a boy. It's a good job we're not short of a penny, or she'd have to walk around in her underwear.' Hetty pulled the dress over her head and stood in nothing but her pink corselet and stockings while she hung it in her wardrobe. 'Bert says the strike is inevitable because of the Triple Alliance. I heard your Percy was involved in the strike committee at the docks, so I thought you might know what was going on.'

Did everyone in Southampton know Percy's business? If they did, once this strike business had blown over, he was going to find it difficult getting any shifts at all. The foremen didn't like troublemakers, and anyone involved in the strike was going to be labelled that way.

'I doubt I know any more than you do. Whatever happens, though, there's nothing we can do about it. And we'll get by somehow, we always do. There will likely be some kind of strike pay from the unions. Heaven knows we've paid them enough in union dues. If not, it'll be the pawnbrokers, not that we have anything much to pawn.' Laura laughed, although it wasn't funny.

'Well, don't be afraid to ask if you need help. It'll give me an excuse for a new dress or two, and I know what it's like to struggle. We didn't always live like this, you know.' Hetty waved her hand to indicate the comfortable looking bed with its quilted counterpane, the green glass dressing table set and the array of beautiful dresses in the open wardrobe.

'No doubt it'll all be a flash in the pan. If not, we can

probably all live on the vegetables from Dad's garden.'

'How is your dad?' Hetty closed the wardrobe door and picked up the grey linen day dress she'd been wearing when Laura arrived. 'Last time you were here you said his back was playing up again.'

'He's fine now. He's been getting Stanley to help him out in the garden. At least it gets him away from Maria and Mum. They're spoiling him rotten. She never let any of us get away with a thing, but Stanley can do no wrong. Between them they're turning him into a right sissy.'

'Well, it can't be easy for the poor lad losing his father like that. Before I met Bert, my George suffered terribly for want of a father. Not that you'd know it to see him now, of course.' Hetty slipped the dress over her head and straightened her hair in the mirror. 'Is Maria any better now? I can't imagine how she'll ever get over what happened to her Fred, especially knowing whoever killed him is still out there somewhere. I swear I wouldn't be able to sleep at night.'

'She's coping, I think. If Fred had died in an accident, like Lizzie's first husband, George, it'd probably be easier, but it's been over a year. I doubt they're going to catch anyone now, unless whoever did it has a sudden fit of conscience and confesses.'

'They found fingerprints in the bakery, didn't they?'

'Yes, they found some inside the cash box, but they didn't match any they had in their files, or so they said. Either the chap who broke into the bakery has never done that kind of thing before, or else he's never been caught.'

'Maybe he will be arrested for something one day, and then they'll be able to prove he was the man who killed Fred.'

'Maybe, but it won't bring him back, will it?'

'No, but it might make poor Maria feel better to know he'd been hanged. If someone killed my Bert, I'd want to watch them hang. In fact, I'd want to put the rope around their neck myself.'

Goodness, Hetty Porter could talk the hind legs off a donkey, but she was a good customer and Laura had received another order and a shilling tip from her, so she couldn't really complain. What with the money she'd earned this morning and the advance for this latest job, they'd be flush this week. She might even have enough to put a little something in the emergency tin.

7 - Saturday 1 May 1926

When Lenny left work, men were gathered in a knot outside the dock gate. It looked like a mother's meeting but he knew they were all talking about the strike. It was the only topic of conversation lately. The union was still trying to come to an agreement and rumours were flying like sparks round a bonfire. Much as he hoped it wouldn't come to it, a strike seemed unavoidable. He spotted Percy at once. With his bulk, his scar and the way he favoured his good leg, he was hard to miss. Hopefully, his presence meant he'd had at least one shift today. If the strike went ahead, they were going to need every penny to pay the rent and buy food. Arthur Fisk was there, too, whispering furtively to Jimmy Pothecary. At least Percy wasn't huddled with them. It was better he kept away from those two. He got in enough trouble all on his own. Harry Smith looked to be concluding one of his rousing speeches. Lenny couldn't hear him properly, but it was almost certainly some Bolshevik nonsense.

Percy saw Lenny and broke away from the group. 'Fancy a pint before we go home?'

'I'd rather get my wages back to Laura in one piece.'

Surprisingly, Percy didn't put up a fight. He waved to the others, said, 'See you later, boys,' and fell into step with Lenny.

They crossed the railway tracks and the road and then walked along the edge of Queen's Park in companionable silence. The sun danced through the new leaves and the first flowers had begun to erupt in the borders. The splashes of colour put Lenny in mind of Monet. It was a world away from the drab warehouses and cranes of the docks. They were more like Lowry. Their only real colour came from the ever-changing sea and sky. If he had to choose, he'd take Monet any day.

'So, did you get a shift today?' he asked Percy, as they turned onto Terminus Terrace. 'Only we could do with the money if there really is a strike coming.'

'You worry too much.' Percy reached into his inside pocket, pulled out a small roll of banknotes and unfurled them. 'There's five quid here, four for Lor and one for me. That should keep us going for a while.'

'Where the hell did you get all that?' Lenny stared at the five slightly crumpled and grubby pound notes. They looked real enough, but he'd have had to work two weeks of full days to earn that much.

'Mostly helping with a bit of cargo redistribution for Arthur Fisk.' Percy raised his eyebrows mysteriously, rolled the money up and shoved it back into his pocket.

'Pilfering?' Lenny frowned. 'For pity's sake, Percy, do you want to be out of work or what?'

'There was no pilfering at all on my part, Len. All I was doing was moving crates from one place to another and asking no questions. Isn't that exactly what I'm paid to do?'

Lenny was saved from answering when Harry Smith caught up with them. Although he was the shop steward and well respected, he was the sort of chap you'd walk past in the street without noticing. He cultivated an air of ordinariness; average height, biscuit-brown hair, clean-shaven and, from his flat cap to his work boots, dressed without the slightest flourish. It made him easy to miss in a crowd, even when you knew him.

'I'm a bit worried about this strike.' He was slightly out of breath from running.

'Aren't we all?' Lenny snorted. 'I've got a wife, two little ones and a great useless lump of a brother-in-law to feed, plus rent to pay.'

'The thing is, I could really do with the help of military men like yourselves, men with experience of the front line. Make no mistake about it, this strike is a war, and most of the others . . . well, they're not experienced, not disciplined.'

For all his averageness, there was something about his voice, an almost mesmeric quality. 'The thing is, there are a few loose cannons. Arthur Fisk and Jimmy Pothecary are the ringleaders. They both have track records. Arthur's desperately trying to live up to his brothers and Jimmy is his father's son. They're too hot headed. The government are going to try to paint us all as lower-class thugs. We need to prove them wrong and keep public support. The last thing we need is trouble on the picket lines. You're quite friendly with the two of them, Percy. I'd like you to be my right-hand man, my eyes and ears, and keep them under control.'

Lenny almost burst out laughing, but he managed to disguise his amusement as a coughing fit. The idea of Percy keeping himself under control, never mind anyone else, would have been comical if the situation wasn't so serious. Then again, maybe it was a stroke of genius on Harry's part to put one of the most likely instigators of trouble in charge of stopping it.

'They just need some discipline instilled in them,' Percy replied, while huffing, puffing and blushing with pleasure. 'You can count on me.'

When they reached the corner of Marsh Lane, Harry turned left, and they turned right past the cattle market to the railway bridge.

'So, you really think this strike is going to happen then?' Lenny said as they climbed the steps of the bridge.

'It has to. The poor bloody miners have been shit on by the mine owners. If we all sit back and watch them cut their wages again and again, never mind the extra hour a day, our bosses will think they can get away with the same. Then where will we be? We barely earn enough to survive as it is. The government doesn't care and the unions are no use. Maybe we do need a revolution to put things right.'

A train rattled beneath them with a hiss of steam and a squeal of brakes. They descended the steps on the far side of the bridge and turned for home. By the time the train had finally passed and conversation was once again possible, their terrace was almost in sight.

'So, you're going to forget about fighting for king and country and join the Bolsheviks now, are you?' Lenny didn't much like the way things were going with the wage cuts, or the way the miners were being treated, but he didn't think Bolshevism, or revolution, was the way forward at all.

'Well, some of the things they say make sense. Why should workers like us toil away for next to nothing, just to line the pockets of the rich? Most of us hardly scrape a living, yet the mine and dock owners all sit in their fine houses, warm and safe with good food in their bellies at our expense. They get rich on the back of our work.'

They sounded more like Harry Smith's words than Percy's.

'And you'd be happy to see the king and queen dragged onto the street and executed, just like the Russian Tsar? Is that the kind of country you fought for? It sure as hell wasn't why I went to France.'

'Look around you, Len. Is this the land fit for heroes they promised us? Do you think the miners who dug all those tunnels in France feel like heroes now?'

Lenny surveyed the grimy street of cramped and damp

terraced houses. Like the docks, it could have been a Lowry painting, all grey, black and burnt sienna. The giant gasometers in their rusty metal cradles loomed over them, casting a dark shadow across the dusty road. A group of lads in patched shorts kicked a battered football against the front walls of the houses. Amongst them he spotted the tow-haired head of his son, Bobby. The acrid pall of coal smoke caught at the back of his throat and made him cough. Percy did have a point.

8 - Monday 3 May 1926

Harry, Percy and Lenny were huddled together in the darkest, quietest corner of the Railway Tavern, three pints of beer on the table in front of them. The shift had only just ended and the bar was almost empty. The bare boards were freshly spread with sawdust and the tables had been polished to a dull sheen. Percy had insisted they go to the pub to talk about organising pickets, even though Lenny would rather have gone straight home to let Laura know what was going on. His stomach was rumbling, but at least this way he could keep an eye on Percy and maybe stop him going overboard with the drink.

'I don't think I'll have any problem getting pickets together.' Harry stroked his stubbly chin. 'My only concern is making sure there's no trouble.'

'Don't worry about it.' Percy took a swig of his drink. 'I can handle Fisk and his gang. I've got the measure of them.'

As if on cue, Arthur and a crowd of other young men, mostly in their early twenties, swaggered into the pub all bluff and bravado. Despite his confidence, it looked as if Percy was going to have his work cut out. They were loud, boisterous and full of themselves. Lenny was glad no one was expecting him to keep them under control.

'The troops have arrived, boss.' Arthur stood at the table with his hands on his hips. He appeared to be the spokesperson for the group. His dark hair was swept back from his forehead, and though he had a baby face, he was all biceps and fists. There were a lot of young men like him these days. They'd been too young to fight in the war and had chips on their shoulders and a desperate need to prove themselves.

There was a flurry of movement as chairs were rearranged and trips made back and forth to the bar. Harry drummed his fingers impatiently on the table until, finally, everyone was ready. 'As you know,' he began. 'The government subsidy has ended. The miners have been locked out and had their contracts terminated. They have rejected the extra hour and the pay cut, just as we all knew they would. The government has declared war on the working classes, and we, along with the printers, iron and steel workers, builders, electricity and gas workers, railway men and road transport workers, are on strike as of one minute to midnight tonight. Bevan has asked us all to fight for the soul of labour and the salvation of the miners. Are we all ready to support them?'

'Not a minute on the day or a penny off the pay.' Arthur raised his fist and his voice. 'We're armed and ready to defend the miners and start the revolution.'

A murmur of approval went up from the other young men. Lenny looked around the table. What had he got himself into? Harry mentioned war and they acted as if it was all a game, but if they were suddenly transported to the trenches in France, they'd probably wet their pants.

'Gentlemen!' Harry shook his head sadly. 'As I keep trying to tell you, we have to be prepared to be in this for the long haul. Hotheads don't win wars. They're won by restraint, organisation and strategy. We need to present a rational, cohesive force, and to that end, I have put Percy here in charge of the pickets. His experience in France is going to be invaluable.'

'What use is an old man with a gammy leg?' Arthur looked petulantly down his nose at Percy. 'No offence, but it's young, fit men like us you need. Men who can come down hard on the blacklegs and make them think twice.'

Harry let out a long, slow breath and rubbed at his temples. 'What I need is men who can obey orders without question. If you can't do that, you may as well leave now.'

'Oh, Arthur.' Percy surprised Lenny by smiling indulgently rather than rising to the insults. 'War is mostly a waiting game. If you'd been in France, like your three brothers, you'd know that. If they'd come back they'd have told you all about sitting for months in muddy trenches filled with rats and lice. Luckily for you, you won't have to do that. No one will be shooting at you or trying to blow you up, and you won't have to stand on a bloody fire step all night watching nothing happen through a periscope.

'You might think pushing thirty is old, but being young and

fit isn't the be-all and end-all. I was your age when I got blown up, but some of the best soldiers I met were older men. They had patience. They weren't impetuous like me. If I'd listened a bit harder and been a bit less full of myself, I might have stayed in one piece like Lenny here. We were all eager to get stuck into the fighting when we got over there, just like you are now, but we had to learn to be disciplined and do what we were told. We might not have liked the generals or the officers, we might not have even trusted they always knew what they were doing, but if we'd ignored them and gone charging into No Man's Land before they told us to, we'd have lost the war and you'd be speaking fucking German now.'

Arthur scowled, but the eyes of all the other young men were now fixed on Percy. Lenny could almost see their swagger evaporating and their respect growing. He'd never been so proud of Percy in his life. Perhaps all this strike stuff was just what he needed.

9 - Tuesday 4 May 1926

Laura climbed the steps of the railway bridge with her head a mass of conflicting thoughts and worries. Most of them revolved around Percy. Didn't they always? Only two years separated them, so they'd always been close. Lizzie, Maria and Willy were so much older, and Ethel was such a timid mouse. It often felt like her and Percy against the world. They'd been alike once, too, filled with confidence, mischief and enthusiasm. Then he came back from France broken in body and mind. That was when all the drinking and fighting started. It was as if he were set on a course of self-destruction, either trying to drown his sorrows or obliterate them.

Now he'd got himself involved with the Bolsheviks and some kind of thieving at the docks. The money he'd given her was more than welcome, especially now there was a strike, but stealing from the docks wasn't likely to end well, any more than the strike was. Still, now he was organising the pickets he stood a little straighter and had a look of purpose about him. He was almost like the old Percy; full of ambition and hope. She didn't approve of what he was doing, or how he was standing in the limelight so openly, but she had to admit the change in him was a positive one. Her mother always said she could find a silver lining in a thunderhead on a washday morning. It was true, but it sometimes took a lot of hard work.

She stopped in the middle of the bridge, rubbed at the knots in the small of her back and looked over the wall at the tangle of railway lines. The rough bricks were damp against her hands and the streets below were quieter than usual. The buses, trams and trains weren't running. She'd missed the regular rattle of the latter passing the back of the house this morning, even though they usually annoyed her. There was little else to show a strike was taking place. Washing was blowing on the lines in the gardens of the terraced houses as usual. If the track didn't curve quite so much, she might be able to see the line in her own tiny backyard. The sun was out. A gentle breeze ruffled her hair. Her washing would soon dry, but the direction of the wind meant everything would be covered in smuts from the gasworks by the time she got it in. All that pounding and rinsing and wrestling with the stiff handle of her mother's old mangle was probably for nothing.

With a sigh, she left the bridge, passing the cattle market and heading along Terminus Terrace. The railway station was strangely quiet, with none of the usual bustle of carriages and people going in and out of the arched doorways. She glanced at the clock above the station sign. It was almost two o'clock. She hurried on, past the edge of the park to the road. A crowd had gathered at the dock gate. There were far more pickets than she'd expected, but they looked peaceful, which was a relief. She'd half expected fighting and shouting, especially with Percy in charge.

She picked out Lenny right away. He was easily the tallest man there, and he was probably the thinnest, too. With all the transport workers on strike, the road and the railway tracks were deserted. As she crossed, she noticed Percy talking to that Fisk chap. He was the one who'd got Percy involved in the thieving, or so Lenny said. He was wearing a brown madras checked suit with a matching cap and spotted silk cravat, and he looked dressed for a night on the town. What a pompous arse.

Lenny saw her and waved. He looked pale and drawn, all angular bones and tightly stretched skin. She worried about him. He still had a cough, although he tried to hide it, and he'd lost weight, as if he had any to spare. Percy had a lot to answer for, dragging him out in the rain the other week. He should be at home resting not hanging about the dock gate with all the pickets.

'I thought you might be hungry, so I bought you some food.' She reached into her basket and fished out thick slices of bread and dripping wrapped in a muslin cloth.

'You're an angel.' He took the package from her gratefully. 'My stomach thought my throat had been cut. I'm famished.'

He was always famished.

'I thought you might have come home earlier. It's not as if you're getting paid to picket, and there looks to be more than enough other folk here already, unless Percy's organising a revolution?'

'He says most of them came this morning so they could say they were here for the first day. The longer this goes on the more trouble he's going to have persuading people to turn out, especially early in the morning or during the night.'

Percy had seen her and wandered over to join them. 'Oh, food! Did you bring me some or is it just Lenny you're trying to feed up?' He peered into her basket.

'It's only Lenny that needs it. Unlike you, he doesn't have a beer belly.' She prodded at Percy's midriff, as if he really had a roll of fat there, then fished out a second packet of bread and dripping.

'Pot and kettle,' he laughed. 'Seriously, though, thanks Lor, you're a lifesaver. This picketing is harder work than it looks.'

'Right, standing around all day chatting is hard work. You should have stayed at home and done the laundry if you wanted to know about hard work. I'd have been happy enough to take your place here, not that it looks like you need any extra help.'

'It was a much better turn out than I expected.' Percy looked around at the crowd with a proud smile. 'To be honest, I was just about to tell Len to stand down. There's no point so many of us being here now. I doubt anything much is going to happen today. You might as well go home and enjoy your food in peace.'

*

Instead of going straight home, Lenny led Laura to a bench in the middle of the park near the General Gordon memorial. The area was sheltered from the slight chill of the breeze and far enough away from the crowded dock gates to feel fairly peaceful.

'Honestly, Laura, I'm so starved I don't think I'd have made it home.' He unwrapped the bread and began devouring it hungrily.

'At least it looks as though things have gone along without any trouble. I was half afraid to come for fear of what I might find.' She arched her back and stretched, pleased to be off her feet for a while. The park was pretty, with new green leaves on the trees and the first spring flowers brightening the borders. They rather made up for the memorial, which, with its polished pink granite columns, looked as if someone had dumped a giant candlestick holder on a mound of grass.

'Yes, it didn't go too badly at all,' Lenny said through a mouthful of bread. 'There was a moment or two, when a group of posh lads started taunting us. They said they were getting organised to take over our jobs and break the strike. I thought it was going to turn nasty, but Percy was a marvel. He saw them coming across the park and gave a wonderful speech to all the pickets.'

'Our Percy talking sense?' Laura looked at him as if he'd gone mad. 'That must be a first.'

'You should have heard him, Laura. He said to ignore them because they were just a bunch of boys who knew nothing about dock work. He said, "They've never done a real day's work in their lives. Five minutes and they'll be wanting to go home to their mothers, and if by some miracle they don't, they're likely to do more harm than good." They were all dressed in fancy suits, and by the looks of them, most were college types, maybe from the Hartley College. Our boys lapped it up. They jeered and booed, of course, and called them blacklegs, but there was no violence, not one bit.'

'Maybe Percy's finally found his calling.' She laughed and rested her head on Lenny's shoulder. 'Although I must admit, I'd have had him down for starting the trouble rather than stopping it.'

10 - Wednesday 5 May 1926

It was odd to see the town at this time of night; empty and quiet with barely a light in a window. The pubs had been closed for a couple of hours and even the slowest of the drunks had made their way home. For once, Percy was stone-cold sober, which added to the strangeness. Usually, he saw these night-time streets through a drunken, distorted haze. As he walked towards the docks with Lenny, stepping from one puddle of lamplight to the next, their footsteps seemed to echo on the deserted pavements.

'So, they don't know we're coming, then?' Lenny spoke in a whisper, as if afraid of waking someone.

Percy shook his head. Why was Lenny always so concerned about other people? 'I want to check up on them. Arthur Fisk, Jimmy Pothecary and Sam Strange were suspiciously keen to do the night picket, and I don't trust them. Fisk has been whining about all the money he's losing from his black-market activities, and I get the idea they're planning to sneak into the warehouses and help themselves to whatever they can lay their hands on while there's no one about.'

'You didn't mind when they were paying you to move stuff around for them.' Lenny shot him a cynical, sideways look.

'That's different,' Percy replied. Lenny's blind spot on the matter annoyed him. He'd tried to make him see it was a victimless crime, at least in as much as any crime could be. Only the dock owners lost out and, given how badly they paid their workers, they deserved to. Besides, they didn't realise they were losing out and what they didn't know couldn't hurt them. No matter how many times he said it, Lenny still sucked his teeth and shook his head, as if he had committed the crime of the century.

'Len, I keep telling you; the foreman knew exactly what was going on. In fact, he was making sure all the paperwork tallied up and nothing was missed. There are a lot more people in on it than just Fisk and his mates. The only reason they got me involved was the need to move as much as they could before the strike. It's been going on for years, and they all know exactly how much they can get away with. If Fisk and his boys start making off with stuff now, though, there'll be no one to cover it up, and they're bound to blame the pickets.'

'I'm not sure the two of us will be able to do much if they're in there helping themselves. Perhaps we should have brought Harry with us?'

There was a hint of anxiety in Lenny's eyes. It reminded Percy of the trenches. Those stupid lads were nothing to be scared of, though. Surely Lenny could see that? Maybe it was just nervousness. He wasn't a coward, after all. He just worried too much about doing the right thing.

The South Western Hotel was now in sight. The breeze

blowing off the water was chillier than he'd expected. He turned up the collar of his jacket against the cold.

'Harry put me in charge of the pickets for a reason. I know what I'm doing, don't you worry. Fisk is the ringleader. The others just follow along. I can take him with one hand tied behind my back. Once he's under control the rest will follow.'

'If you say so.' Lenny turned towards the dock gate, where a small group of young men in flat caps were gathered. Two bored looking constables were leaning against the wall of the Docks Post Office some distance from them, smoking and half watching. Neither seemed particularly interested in what the men were doing and, with the likelihood of blacklegs or trouble slim, it was no wonder.

Lenny and Percy's necks still snapped to the right and left in a kind of reflex action as they crossed the road and the rails, even though there was no traffic at this time of night and no trains were running because of the strike. Percy eyed the men. Just as he'd thought, Arthur Fisk was nowhere to be seen. He knew the little ratbag would get up to something as soon as his back was turned. Then he spotted Sam and Jimmy. If Arthur really did plan on moving some goods, he'd have thought he'd need them with him. He strode purposefully up to Sam, a skinny lad with ginger hair, a weak chin and ears that looked as if his mother might have used them to carry him around. The youngest of the three and not exactly blessed when it came to brains, he was the most likely to spill the beans.

'Where's Arthur?'

A look of fear passed across Sam's vacant face. 'I . . . I . . . don't rightly know.' He blinked slowly and looked towards Jimmy for help. At least he might have been looking at Jimmy. One of his eyes had a mind of its own.

Something was definitely going on.

'He's going to be late.' Jimmy was more confident, almost insolent. 'He broke a window and cut his hand on the glass. He'll be along soon, though.'

Percy stared at him. A year or so older than Sam, he was more intelligent and good looking in a roguish way. His long, thin face was dominated by thick brows that met in the middle, a small, tight mouth and hair like treacle toffee that stuck up despite the oil he used to control it. How much of this story was the truth? Both of them looked shifty, but if Arthur was in the warehouse thieving why weren't they with him? Percy didn't buy the story and he could see from Lenny's face that he didn't, either. He looked beyond the men towards the quiet, dark docks. The gates were shut and there was no sign of movement within, but there were plenty of ways to sneak inside and a huge area in which to hide if you did. Without going in himself, there was no way of checking if Arthur was in there.

He was about to walk away when Jimmy nodded towards the park. 'There he is now. Better late than never, eh?'

Percy turned and sure enough, Arthur was strolling towards them, all dressed up in his checked suit and seemingly without a care in the world. So, he hadn't been in the warehouses after all.

'Sorry I'm late,' he said when he finally made it across the road. 'I smashed a beer bottle and managed to cut my hand clearing it up. Took me a while to pick the glass out and wrap it up.' He held up his right hand, which was covered in a fresh, slightly bloody bandage.

'A beer bottle you say?' Percy glanced towards Sam and Jimmy. They both shuffled their feet sheepishly. Sam's face had turned bright red and he looked as if he might burst into tears. 'Jimmy said it was a window.'

Arthur frowned and shot Jimmy a dirty look. 'No, it was definitely a beer bottle.' He took a packet of cigarettes out of his pocket and offered them around.

'Sorry about that, I must have misunderstood.' Jimmy took a cigarette with a nervous glance at Arthur. 'Still, window, bottle, what does it matter? He cut his hand and he's here now.'

Satisfied there was no pilfering going on, at least so far, Percy and Lenny headed towards home. They were passing beneath the streetlamp in front of the Terminus Station before either of them spoke.

'What did you make of that?' Percy glanced sideways at Lenny. The bottle-window thing seemed fishy to him, but Lenny was the brains where he was the brawn, and he valued his opinion.

'The three of them were up to something, I'm sure,' Lenny said. 'I don't think any of them had been in the warehouses, but all that business about windows and bottles and the way they looked . . .' He blew out his cheeks. 'There was definitely something going on.'

That was exactly what Percy thought. He just wished he knew what it was.

11 - Wednesday 5 May 1926

The butcher's shop smelt of sawdust and blood. Laura looked longingly at the legs of lamb and racks of pork ribs in the window. What a feast they'd make, if only she could afford them. Unfortunately, she'd have to content herself with pig's trotters.

'Some nice meaty ones if you can, Mr Robinson.'

'My trotters are all meaty, Mrs McAllen.' Mr Robinson wiped his huge hands on his bloody apron and laughed. He was all rosy cheeks and thinning hair that looked as if the top of his head was trying to escape from a moth-eaten sable hat. As if to make up for the lack of hair on the top of his head, he'd grown a luxuriant moustache. 'I'll pick you out the best ones all the same. How many do you want?'

'Four should be enough for a nice stew to keep us going for a few days. I wondered if there'd be any left, what with the strike and everyone having to tighten their belts.'

'Well, it's been quiet, that's for sure. Everyone's afraid to spend money.' He picked out four fat, pink trotters, added another for good measure and wrapped them up in paper. 'I put an extra one in for your men on the picket line. No charge. Keep it under your hat, though. I don't want everyone expecting it. Those poor bloody miners. I'm glad someone is standing up for them. My granddad was a miner, you know, down in Cornwall in the tin mines.'

He patted her hand as he passed over the package. For such a large, jolly man, he was surprisingly gentle.

'It's going to be hard on you, too, if the strike goes on.' Laura passed over her coins and put the packet in her basket. 'Not many people round here have any savings to see them through.'

'Don't you worry about me. People have still got to eat, so I'll get by. I'm not so sure about poor old George Jones, though.' He stroked his moustache sadly. 'Buggers broke into his shop last night, smashed a window, got in and made off with loads of tobacco and cigarettes. They more or less cleared the place out, and they emptied his cash box. To add insult to injury, one of them must have cut himself on the glass and bled all over the show as well.'

'Oh, that's too bad. He's such a nice man. Percy buys his fags there.'

'Well, you tell Percy to keep his eyes peeled for anyone selling off cheap ones. I hope the buggers give themselves away.'

*

When Laura got home with the shopping, Lenny and Percy were at the kitchen table drinking tea. Stubble-faced, they couldn't stop rubbing their bleary eyes. They'd both slept in after their late night on the picket line and she'd left them to it. She put the bread and eggs she'd bought into the larder then got the large stockpot out of the kitchen cabinet and filled it with water.

'I hope you two aren't going to sit around here all day like piffy getting in my way.' She rinsed the pig's trotters under the tap and put them in the pot.

'Bloody hell, Lor, give us a rest.' Percy had his elbow on the table and his head propped on his hand. 'We've been up half the night.'

'Well, I wish someone would give me a bloody rest.' Laura put the pot on the range.

'It's not all fun and games on the picket line, you know,' Percy said. 'We're not all standing about smoking and drinking and having a laugh.'

'Well, you won't be doing much smoking, that's for sure.' Laura gave the trotters a stir and put the lid on the pot. 'Some bugger smashed the window of Jones's tobacconist last night, stole all his stock and emptied his cash box. Robinson, the butcher, told me to tell you to keep your eyes peeled for anyone trying to sell nicked fags. They'll probably be covered in blood, too, because the idiot cut himself on the glass.'

Percy straightened up and looked at Lenny. 'Well, that might explain what Fisk was up to.'

Lenny frowned back. 'I wouldn't put it past him.'

Percy raised his eyebrows. 'The coppers are too busy watching the pickets, and he has been whining about all the money he's losing because of the strike.'

'Putting a few crates or sacks onto a little rowboat instead of a cargo hold or a warehouse is a bit different from breaking and entering, though.' Lenny scratched his chin. 'Especially a shop on his own doorstep, where he'd risk being recognised. Surely even he isn't that stupid.'

'Brazen more like. He did have a cut hand, and there was something decidedly suspicious about how he got it. He was flashing around the fags, too, and he's not normally one for sharing. Maybe I should go and have a word with George Jones. He's such a nice chap, he doesn't deserve to be robbed of his livelihood.'

'We could be jumping to conclusions, though.' Lenny rubbed his thumb across his bottom lip. 'It might all be a coincidence.'

Laura joined them at the table with a sigh. 'I like George Jones as much as anyone, but I think you two should stay out of it.'

A cut hand, a packet of cigarettes and a vague feeling something was dodgy didn't seem enough of a reason for stirring up trouble to her. Fisk was an idiot, but even idiots deserved the benefit of the doubt.

12 - Thursday 6 May 1926

The salmon-pink dawn light washed over the sunny side of the trench, while the shadows remained deepest cobalt shot with violet. Swirls of mist crept along the ground and mingled with the smoke from the bursting shells of the Hun's morning hate. It was funny how little the shells bothered Lenny now. Since Percy got hit he'd developed a kind of fatalism about them. No matter what you did, they'd either hit you or they wouldn't, so there was no point worrying about them. Then he caught a mustardy whiff and began to cough. At almost the same moment, Corporal Brodrick shouted, 'Gas!'

Despite burning, streaming eyes and a choking, spluttering cough, he fumbled into his gas mask in a panic. The shells might not hold any more terror, but gas was everyone's worse nightmare. Even with the mask on, he couldn't stop coughing, and each ragged inhalation seemed to bring less and less air. He fell to his knees, gasping and spluttering, terrified he would drown in his own tears, snot and phlegm. He remembered Dougie's horrified face as he'd sunk beneath the Passchendaele mud, his friend's slimy hands slipping from his grip. He'd drowned despite all their efforts to save him. Drowning in mud was a ghastly way to go, but so was suffocating in your own gas mask.

Instinct made him claw at the mask to rip it off, even though logic told him this was madness. Joe grabbed his hands and pulled them away from his face. Was it Joe or was it Corporal Brodrick? With his eyes streaming and everyone in gas masks, he couldn't be sure. They were both the same size and it was hard to tell one from the other through the fogged glass. He couldn't get any air. The last thing he saw was Joe turning towards Corporal Brodrick – or Corporal Brodrick turning to Joe – and shaking his head and drawing his hand across his throat.

*

Lenny clawed his way to wakefulness. He was coughing, spluttering and gasping for breath, as if he really had just been gassed. For a second or two, he even thought he could smell mustard. He sat up and rubbed his eyes. Daylight streamed through the shabby curtains. The old mattress that served as Bobby and Gladys's bed was empty. Their blankets and sheets lay in an untidy heap on the floor. He stared at the peeling wallpaper speckled with spots of black mould and coughed some more. This place was better than the rooms they'd rented in the house in St Denys. It was less cramped, less damp and had no cockroaches, at least not any he'd seen. As improvements go, though, it was hardly a giant leap. Still, without Percy and his little bit of pension money, they'd never have been able to afford to move. He'd hoped to find somewhere even better this year, maybe away from the railway lines and all the smoke and soot of the gasworks, but this blasted strike made it unlikely they'd be able to afford to move again any time soon. The money Laura hid in the old cocoa tin in the back of the cupboard wasn't going to last long with just strike pay to live on.

He had no idea what the time was, but he could hear pots and pans crashing about in the kitchen below. Had Percy left yet? Last night, when he'd said he was going to check up on the pickets first thing, he'd sounded like a general preparing to inspect his troops. No one could say he wasn't taking his picket organising duty seriously. The responsibility seemed to be doing him a power of good. He was the happiest he'd been in ages, and he'd stayed sober all week, too, which could only be a bonus. He had his work cut out keeping control of Fisk and his mates, though. They were too full of themselves and eager to fight for Lenny's liking. Whether or not they were involved in the burglary at the tobacconists, they were definitely up to something dodgy, and it was only a matter of time before they came unstuck. If Percy had any sense he'd distance himself from them as much as possible. But Percy and sense were strange bedfellows.

He heard steps on the creaking stairs. Then Laura came into the room with a chipped mug in her hand and her eyes full of concern. 'I heard you coughing and made you some chamomile tea.' She put the steaming mug on the old crate they used as a bedside table.

'What time is it?'

'Half past nine. Bobby and Gladys have gone to school and Percy has gone off to the docks. You were coughing a lot again last night so we let you sleep.'

'I can't seem to shake it. It's always the same since I got gassed. Every little cold and sniffle ends up in a cough that just won't go. Sodding Germans and their poisonous gas.'

'Look on the bright side. If it wasn't for the gas you wouldn't have been sent home to recover, Percy wouldn't have gone to visit you and you wouldn't have met me.'

'In that case, I take it all back.' He smiled and grabbed her hand, pulling her down onto the bed beside him. She snuggled into the crook of his arm with a soft sigh and tugged at the blanket, bringing it up to her chin. He kissed the top of her head.

'I'm supposed to be going to visit Mum later.' She reached down and began to pull at the already straining cord of his pyjama bottoms. 'Still, it isn't often we have the house to ourselves, so it would be a shame to waste it.'

'Even the strike has its good side.' He gasped as her cool hand met his warm flesh.

13 - Thursday 6 May 1926

A solid line of blue-black uniforms and tall helmets dominated the dock gate. The constables outnumbered the pickets. Shoulder-to-shoulder with them, the specials, in ordinary suits, striped armbands and tin hats, stood grim faced. Percy's heart beat a little faster when he saw them from across the park. There could only be one reason for them to turn out in such numbers. They were expecting trouble. He'd known this day was coming but not when. The specials were part of the Organisation for the Maintenance of Supplies. The unions had issued permits to the O.M.S. to move food from the docks, and Harry said they should let them. They wouldn't keep the public support if there were food shortages. Percy had done everything he could to prepare his men. But would they remember everything he'd told them?

As far as he could tell, the strike breakers were most likely to be students. They were no real threat. According to the *British Worker*, students from Oxford University were being coerced with promises of higher grades if they volunteered, so most of them were only doing it to get better marks in their exams. Would the pickets remember this, stand fast and act like reasonable men fighting for a reasonable cause? Arthur Fisk, Jimmy Pothecary and Sam Strange were amongst them, so it could just as easily end up with a mass brawl. If he'd known the O.M.S. was coming today, he'd have got Lenny out of bed.

Fisk was the biggest danger. If he could distract him and get him on the back foot, he might be able to divide and conquer. He was still wearing that stupid checked suit and cap with the spotted scarf around his neck. He probably thought it made him look good. In reality, it made him look like an idiot who was trying too hard to be something he wasn't. That was half his trouble. He'd watched his brothers go off to war and not come back, and for all his bluff and bravado, he knew he'd never get out of their shadow. Percy made a beeline for him. A few mind games were in order.

'How's the cut?' He nodded at the bandage on Fisk's hand. It was dirty grey now and the dried blood was a rusty shade of brown. Maybe his wound would make him less keen to fight. Then again, everyone knew how much Arthur liked a ruck, as long as he was in no danger of getting hurt.

'It's fine,' he shrugged. 'Just a bit sore, nothing I can't handle.'

'No redness, then?' Percy raised an eyebrow. 'Because when it starts to get red and hot, it's a sure sign of infection. I've seen men in the trenches lose a hand from a silly little cut.'

'Not really.' Arthur shook his head, but there was a hint of worry in his eyes. 'Just a bit sore.'

'Well, as long as you keep it clean and keep an eye on it you should be fine. It's a good job it was a bottle, really.' Percy let his smile turn to a grimace. 'The medics at the front always said a bottle was the best thing to get cut with. They're usually pretty sterile, you see, less chance of tetanus. You've heard of tetanus?'

'Um, sort of.' Arthur swallowed several times.

'Well, it doesn't really matter, seeing as it was a bottle. Now, if it had been a window, like Jimmy said, that would be a whole different kettle of fish. They say window glass is one of the worst things to cut yourself on. It's usually filthy and riddled with the sort of germs that cause tetanus. Of course, door glass is even worse, all those grubby hands touching it all the time. The chances of getting tetanus from the glass in a door is huge.' He paused and looked into Arthur's wide eyes. He was breathing fast and licking his lips. Time for the coup de grâce. 'It's such a horrible way to die. The toxin gets into your system and slowly your muscles start to clench. It usually starts with your jaw muscle, that's why they call it lockjaw, then it moves to your neck and shoulders – and then you can't breathe. It's agony, or so they say. Still, you don't really have to worry about any of that.'

'So, is there any cure for it?' Arthur rubbed at his jaw and wiggled it from side to side. It looked like he was testing it still worked.

'They used to give us injections at the field hospitals. With all those bodies rotting everywhere, they couldn't be too careful. Once the clenching starts, though, it's usually too late.'

By this time, Percy was struggling not to laugh. Arthur looked green around the gills and rubbed anxiously at the edge of his moustache. Percy thought it looked as if it was drawn on with a pencil, and he imagined he'd rub it off if he kept at it. He was as certain as could be that Fisk had cut his hand on a window, probably the window of the tobacconist's door. It might have been a touch cruel to frighten him so much, but at least he wouldn't be thinking about fighting when the O.M.S. crowd arrived.

*

When the lorry finally did pull up and a group of about ten students scrambled out of the back, they were something of an anti-climax. The mass of young men wore pristine suits, crisp, white, collarless shirts and brand-new flat caps. They looked like a bunch of men dressed up as dockers for a play. Percy's first reaction was to laugh. Beside him, Jimmy snorted and there were several other sniggers from the pickets. Even the constables had smiles on their faces.

'Bloody hell,' Jimmy said. 'They look like they've been in Mummy and Daddy's dressing up box. You were right, Percy, none of that lot will last five minutes humping sacks and crates about.'

14 - Thursday 6 May 1926

Mum had gone to put the kettle on and see if Dad wanted his tea in the garden or indoors. This left Laura and Maria alone in the living room in an awkward silence. They'd never been particularly close, except for when they were both pregnant. Maria had been sixteen when Laura was born, and Ethel was six. Apart from sharing the same parents and a bedroom, they had nothing in common. What on earth was taking Mum so long? After forty odd years of marriage, you'd think she'd have run out of things to talk to Dad about. Maria clicked away with her knitting needles. Did she ever move or do anything else? She was making another jumper by the looks of it; blue this time. There must be a limit to how much knitwear one family needed?

Laura looked around the room, desperately trying to think of a topic of conversation. Every object held a memory of some kind, but none were worthy of sharing now. How many times had she watered that aspidistra in the corner? How often and how carefully had she dusted those green ceramic figurines on the mantel, and how many hours had she sat with Lizzie learning to play that piano, or polishing the array of silver cups on top of it?

The carved wooden cigarette box, half hidden behind the cups, conjured memories of sneaking fags with Percy. She must have been about twelve when they first did it, so Percy would have been fourteen. They'd creep down to the bottom of the garden and hide behind the shed to share the spoils. Percy always went first. After a couple of drags, he'd go green and pass the cigarette to her. She'd enjoyed smoking far more than Percy did, but he saw it as a rite of passage and a manly thing to do. Odd how he was the one who still smoked while she could no longer afford to. Dad was always frugal and rationed his cigarette consumption, but he never missed those stolen cigarettes, or, if he did, he never said so.

The memory made her think of the recent break-in. It was something to talk about at least.

'Did you hear about Jones the tobacconist getting burgled on Tuesday night?'

'Oh, my Lord.' Maria looked up from her knitting with such a horrified expression that Laura thought she must have dropped a stitch.

'It sounds like an opportunist kind of thing, what with all the police being tied up with the strike. They got away with most of the stock and emptied the cash box. Poor Mr Jones is such a nice man, too. It's a crying shame.'

'Was he hurt?'

Were those tears in her eyes? Laura suddenly realised how insensitive she'd been to bring up the burglary and the cash box. No wonder Maria was upset. It must have reminded her of what happened to Fred. She wished she'd never mentioned it now.

'No, nothing like that. I don't think Mr Jones found out until the morning. It's probably just young lads, and they'll catch them when they start trying to sell the cigarettes.'

'They never caught the man that killed my Fred.' Maria put her knitting down in her lap and began to rub her hands together anxiously. The way her forehead wrinkled pulled her brows towards the centre of her face. 'It still haunts me that he's out there somewhere. My poor Fred didn't deserve to die like that. I'll never understand why the scoundrel had to hit him over the head. He'd have let him take whatever he wanted. He'd never have risked his life for a tin full of money and a few stale loaves.'

'Of course he wouldn't. Perhaps the man just panicked and went too far by mistake, or maybe he was local, and Fred recognised him. We'll never know, unless they catch him.' Laura felt dreadful for stirring the past up, but it was hard to know what to say to undo it.

'I dream about it, you know.' A tear spilled from Maria's eye and rolled down her cheek. 'I see him there kneading the dough, his hands all covered in flour, getting ready for the day ahead, and then – what must he have been thinking when that man burst in? Did he know he was going to be killed? Was he afraid or in pain?'

'I'm sure it was very quick. He probably didn't have time to think at all, or to know what was happening. Percy says he didn't know he'd been hurt when he got blown up. He felt no pain until afterwards. I'm sure poor Fred didn't suffer.' Even to Laura, every word that came out of her mouth sounded like a useless platitude.

'How can he not have felt any pain when his skull was bashed in? It wasn't just one blow. He was hit over and over again.' Maria closed her eyes, as if she could shut out the horror of the thought.

'You shouldn't think about it too much.'

'How can I stop? Everything I do, everywhere I go, I think about him. I think about those blows raining down on him. I think about him dying all alone and afraid. I think about all the things he will never see while that man is just walking around as if nothing happened.'

15 - Friday 7 May 1926

Lenny huffed on his hands to warm them and raised his face to the sapphire sky. The cool, crisp air filled his lungs and the resulting cough echoed in the empty street. It seemed to bounce around the walls of the terraced houses. With the massive grey cylinders of the gasworks behind him, he could almost imagine the air was clear and clean. Of course, the crumbling terraces told a different story. The squalor and the filth were ground into every brick.

'Looks like it'll be a nice day once the sun warms up.' Percy rubbed his hands together and then fished in his pocket for his cigarettes. 'If we have to stand around on a picket line all morning, at least the weather is being kind to us.'

'Do you think those blackleg students will be there again today? I should quite like to see them all dressed up like costume party dockers.'

Lenny thought they'd make a good painting, maybe in the style of Lowry. Not that he had time for painting these days.

'I think most of them will have trouble getting out of bed this morning.' Percy lit his cigarette and laughed out a plume of smoke. 'It's probably the hardest work the little blighters have ever done in their lives. We could barely jeer for laughing. They thought they were going to have a fine old time playing make believe and heroically moving a few sacks of flour to save the starving poor, or some such nonsense. All they actually achieved was loading and unloading the baggage of other rich people sailing on the Mauretania. It must have been a terrible blow to their pride.'

The door of the Bell and Crown opened, and Amy Medway came out with a dustpan and brush in her hand. She had an emerald-green scarf wrapped around her unruly curls and the sleeves of her dress were rolled up above her elbows. It seemed early to be cleaning her front step, but she crouched and began to sweep. As they got closer, Lenny saw glittering shards of glass on the ground. The chilly air provoked another coughing fit and Amy looked up at the sound.

'Buggers broke into my pub last night.' Her mouth was a hard line and her eyes brimmed with anger. 'I wish I'd heard 'em. I'd have given 'em what for and no mistake.'

'Did they take much?' Lenny bent to help her pick up some of the larger shards of glass.

'I haven't had a chance to check everything yet, but they got last night's takings. It was a good night, too, though I never managed to count the money. I had all the pickets in. They were in fine spirits because they'd got one over on those rich lads. They were telling me all about watching them humping luggage about and not even getting any tips, 'cos the rich passengers didn't want to tip their own kind. Then those buggers went and stole all me takings. I'd have wrung their scrawny necks if I'd caught 'em.'

Lenny stifled a laugh. The thieves had no idea how lucky they were. She'd have wiped the floor with them.

'Do you want me to send a few of the lads to help you clear up and maybe patch up the window?' Percy rubbed his chin and looked through the broken glass into the pub. 'You need to get something up there, even if it's only a bit of board.'

'As long as it's not Fisk or Pothecary. Those useless buggers would probably drink me dry before they'd done any work. And not young Sam Strange, either. I wouldn't trust him to tie his own shoelaces. If he had a thought in his head, it'd be lonely.'

Lenny didn't like the way Amy automatically associated Percy with those three. His reputation for drunkenness and brawling was one thing but being considered part of that crowd was something else entirely, especially if they really were involved in the break-in at the tobacconist's.

Percy didn't seem to mind, though, he just laughed and said, 'I think Tommy Munn's brother Freddie is a glazier. I'll ask if he'll fetch him for you.'

*

As it turned out, Percy was wrong about the blackleg students. They arrived a little after nine. When they jumped out of their lorry, blinking in the sunshine and brandishing their union-issued permits, they looked quite eager and fresh. Either they were more resilient than Percy gave them credit for, or they weren't the same lads who'd carried the luggage the day before. They were certainly dressed just as Percy had described; each a kind of upper-class parody of a docker, with their suits too crisp and their shirts too white. The motley crowd of real dockers stood at the dock gate and jeered them, but there was no trouble. They were only supposed to be moving essential supplies, and the chances were they wouldn't do a good job of it anyway. The row of constables watched uneasily but had no need to intervene. They may have been on opposite sides of the dispute, but apart from a handful of Specials, they were all local men who knew and mostly respected their picket opponents. Some of them might even have felt a sneaking sympathy with the miners. Once the brief interlude of excitement and half-hearted booing had passed, there was little to do but stand around and chat.

Percy soon became engrossed in conversation with Harry Smith, who, until now, had been conspicuous in his absence on the picket line. Lenny caught a few words about a meeting on the Common, but, as most of the chat seemed to be Bolshevik nonsense, he soon lost interest and drifted away from the pair for fear of getting roped into something he'd rather not be involved in. By chance, he found himself standing next to Arthur Fisk and Jimmy Pothecary.

'Did you hear about the trouble in London?' Jimmy's single

shaggy eyebrow shot up towards the peak of his cap. 'The O.M.S. have taken over the buses and trams, and the pickets have been throwing bricks and gawd knows what at them. I heard a couple of buses were overturned and wrecked. One of them came off the road and killed a chap walking past.'

'Where did you hear that?' Lenny wasn't much inclined to believe anything he heard from Jimmy, and he didn't like the delight he seemed to take in it, either. Wasn't violence like that just the kind of thing to turn the public against the strike?

'It was from the BBC on the radio,' Jimmy said with a smug smile.

'We don't have a radio.'

'I could get you a good deal on one if you like.'

'Leave it out.' Arthur elbowed Jimmy in the ribs. 'Ignore him, Lenny. He's full of bull. All he's got is a crystal set, and it don't work half the time, either.'

Up until now, Arthur had been uncharacteristically quiet. Looking at him, Lenny thought he didn't seem well. His face was pasty, his eyes were dull and there was a sheen of sweat on his forehead, as if he had a fever. He was about to ask if he was all right when Jimmy interrupted.

'Bloody hell, that crane is moving.' He pointed towards the dock gate. 'Why are those idiots trying to use the cranes?'

Along with several of the other pickets, he turned to stare towards the water. Sure enough, one of the cranes they used to shift the cargo was moving. He stared at the hook swinging wildly and sucked in a breath. Operating a crane was a skilled job and, in the hands of amateurs, it didn't really bear thinking about.

'Well, I can't see that ending well.' Arthur took off his cap and ran his hand through his hair. 'Silly buggers will end up getting exactly what they deserve.'

'Maybe we should go in and try to stop them before someone gets hurt?' Lenny suggested.

'Nah, let 'em get what's coming to 'em,' Jimmy laughed.

16 - Saturday 8 May 1926

Hetty Porter's parlour always made Laura feel vaguely uncomfortable. She sat on the edge of one of the leather armchairs feeling almost as out of place as the furnishings. It was a modest terraced house and the beautiful, if shabby, chesterfield chairs, polished dark wood dining set and ebony and brass telephone would have looked more at home in a mansion. Since when did working-class people have telephones? Then again, was Hetty really working class, despite where she lived? She was only a couple of years older than Laura, but she'd inherited the house and quite a bit of money from her son's grandmother. She also ran a typing bureau. By Laura's standards, that meant she was rich. She dressed her slightly overblown figure like a woman of means, with her hair always immaculately marcel-waved and her hands soft and unmarked by work. She wasn't at all snobbish, though, and always greeted Laura like an old friend.

What with the men being under her feet so much more than usual and all the dramas of the strike, Hetty's order had taken much longer to finish than Laura would have liked. She'd only managed to put the finishing touches to the second pinafore this morning, after Percy and Lenny went off to the picket line and Bobby and Gladys trotted off to the picture house. Hetty hadn't said a word about how long it had taken. She unwrapped the package, pulled the pinafores out, exclaimed how perfect they were and went to fetch her purse without question. As she waited for her to come back, Laura looked out of the French window at the little garden. The cash would come in handy. There'd be no wage packets coming in this week. If it hadn't been for the extra cash from Percy's dodgy dealings, she'd have been forced to dip into the emergency fund to pay for the picture house.

When Hetty returned with the money, she also carried a large package wrapped in brown paper. 'Now, I don't want you to be offended, but I've made you up a little food parcel.' She handed the package to Laura. 'It's only sugar, tea and cake; that kind of thing. I know your men are on strike, and believe me, I remember what it's like to look down the line of every penny. You know my background. I've never made any secret of the fact I wasn't married when I had George, or that Bert isn't his father. Until George's grandmother found out about us, we barely had a pot to piss in, or food in the cupboard. I had to clean people's houses, and my health was never good. I used to suffer something terrible with my knees and back.'

'I don't think I'm in any position to take offence,' Laura smiled, faintly embarrassed to be a charity case but grateful all the same. 'This bloody strike is the last thing we all need. You know Percy's hardly the most dependable of men, and Lenny, well, he tries hard, but the docks don't pay well.'

'I heard a rumour that Percy was organising the pickets.' Hetty settled into the chair opposite Laura with a kind smile. 'How's that going?'

'It seems the whole world knows Percy's business.' Laura rubbed her brow. At least Hetty hadn't said he was consorting with the communists, although she probably knew about that, too. 'I don't think it's going to make him popular with the bosses when all this is over. The funny thing is, it's done him good. He's stopped drinking and fighting, and he's happier than I've seen him in ages. Sometimes I look at him and wonder where my good-for-nothing brother has gone. He's got his work cut out with some of the pickets, though. One of them is nothing but trouble looking for a place to happen. There was a break-in at the tobacconist's on Northam Road a few days back and Percy thinks he's involved in it somehow. Of course, he has no proof and it's probably best he keeps his nose out of it, even if Mr Jones is a nice old chap and doesn't deserve to be robbed.'

'That's interesting.' Hetty raised her eyebrows. 'You wouldn't be talking about Arthur Fisk by any chance?'

'That's him. Why, do you know something about him?'

'My Bert was only talking about him the other day. It's no secret Bert dabbled in the black market during the war. Well, truth be told, I did, too. They were hard times. We had to do what we could to make ends meet. Of course, these days, he sticks to mending boats, but his cousin, Frank, still runs the little boats into the docks at night. Anyhow, Bert was at the boatyard, on Thursday I think it was, and Arthur Fisk came wandering in looking for Frank. He had a load of cigarettes and tobacco he wanted to offload. Bert told him to sling his hook. "It's one thing selling stuff from the docks," he said, "the men at the top have got more money than sense and they pay their workers a pittance." He was sure this stuff didn't come from the docks, though, and Bert and Frank aren't in the business of fencing stuff stolen from our own kind. It sounds to me like your Percy was right about Fisk.'

'It certainly sounds like he was involved in some way. I'd tell your Bert to be careful, though. I've heard some bad things about Fisk and his cronies.'

'Don't you worry.' Hetty waved her hand dismissively. 'Bert's got the measure of him and his gang. Fisk lost three brothers in the war. Bert says his mother never lets him forget about it, either. The Pothecary lad ended up in the workhouse after his father hanged. As for the other one, Strange, he's a few pennies short of a shilling and does what they tell him. Bert says the trouble with the lot of them is that they feel they missed out on their chance of glory in the war because they were too young. That's why they're running around creating mayhem now. They're trying to prove themselves. The men who went to war, like Bert and your Percy and Lenny, know the truth of it, and Fisk and his friends wouldn't last five minutes up against any of them.'

'Lenny says much the same thing,' Laura nodded. 'Actually, Percy put the wind up Fisk something cruel the other day. Fisk claimed he cut his hand on a broken bottle. Percy thought he might have done it breaking into the tobacconist's, so he fed him a line about people getting tetanus from window glass. He frightened him so much he went and got a tetanus injection at the hospital. It made him so sick he had to be taken home from the picket line on Friday. Serves him right, if he really did break into Mr Jones's shop.'

17 - Sunday 9 May 1926

Given the choice, Lenny would have been slumped in the parlour eating a slice of the sweet, fruity bread pudding that Laura had made this morning. Thinking about the warm sugary smell of it made his mouth water. Going to the Common on Sunday afternoon to listen to Harry Smith talking about communism wasn't exactly his idea of fun, but Percy had dragged him along anyway. Perhaps if the place wasn't packed with thousands of people, being out in the spring sunshine with all the trees coming into leaf might have been pleasant. As it was, they couldn't get anywhere near either of the two stages. Even with his height advantage, Lenny could barely see the speakers, let alone hear them. Percy tried to push his way through the throng and Lenny followed, but they didn't get very far and, as neither of them could work out which stage Harry was on, it was pointless.

'We should have come early and got a place near the front,' Percy grumbled.

'Oh well, we can always ask him what he said later. I'm sure it's nothing we haven't heard before.' Lenny wasn't the slightest bit interested in anything Harry had to say. He didn't believe revolution was the answer to anything.

They both strained their ears and caught the odd word or two. As they were pretty much halfway between the two stages, the two competing speeches meant the gist of both escaped them. Lenny thought he heard something about the Board of Guardians denying benefits to strikers' families. This wasn't news to him, and it was drowned out by boos anyway. The words 'moderation' and 'victory' kept cropping up, and there were big cheers when one of the speakers shouted, 'Your power is immense', and, 'No possibility of defeat.' After a while, trying to work out what was being said was too much, so Lenny gave up straining to listen and watched the crowd instead. They were almost all men like him, in flat caps and shabby working-men's clothes in a palette of dull greens, browns and greys. There were a few women dotted here and there, perhaps wives or shop girls. Some peered intently at the stage, while others were smoking, chatting amongst themselves or looking as bored as Lenny felt. Maybe they'd only come because football and cricket matches were taking place afterwards.

Then someone a few yards to their left began to shout. 'Get back to work, you bloody communists. You're no better than the Hun.'

A wave of pushing and shoving ran through the throng of strikers as they tried to deal with the heckler. For a moment, Lenny thought it might turn into a riot, but it was soon clear the strikers had the measure of the agitator. They knew he was trying to stir up a violent reaction and discredit the strike. Hadn't Harry been warning them all about that very thing from the start? He couldn't see who'd been doing the shouting, but by the movement in the crowd, he could tell there were a few troublemakers, and they were being bundled away from the stages in several different directions.

Percy began to bob his head, trying to see what was going on. As one of the waves of movement got closer to them, Lenny got a glimpse of a group of well-dressed men. They looked as if they were trying to disappear amongst the mass of people, but two of them were being pushed their way. One was short and wiry, with big, gingery side-whiskers that gave him the look of an organ grinder's monkey. The other was taller and had a long face with a pronounced brow and some old, yellowish green bruising, as if he'd already been in a fight. He was wearing a black trilby hat, but it had been knocked to one side by the jostling.

'That's the fascist who caused all the trouble in the Bell and Crown the other week.' Percy began to shove his way towards the man.

'He's trying to start a fight. Don't be suckered into one.' Lenny grabbed at Percy's jacket and tried to pull him back.

To his credit, Percy did stop for a moment, but the men were being pushed towards them anyway. Then the man in the trilby caught sight of Percy. His horrified expression made it clear he recognised him, and his frantic struggle to get away said he didn't want to come face to face with him again. The trilby man's panic transferred itself to the monkey man and within a few moments, they'd both disappeared from view.

'Don't worry, I only want to find out where he goes,' Percy

said, as he started shoving his way towards the place the two men had been.

Lenny did his best to follow. It was all for nothing, though. They did what they could to track the surge in the mass of men, but the fascists had vanished. The only trace they found of them was a battered black trilby right at the edge of the crowd, near the treeline.

18 - Monday 10 May 1926

The police had obviously decided the picketing dockers weren't in any danger of rioting because, this afternoon, there were only four constables at the dock gate. Amongst them, Percy recognised the ruddy face and bulbous nose of his old school mate, Charlie West. Of course, Charlie's nose had been smaller in their school days, before he started drinking.

'How's tricks, Charlie?' He put out his hand and Charlie shook it with a toothy smile.

'Not too bad, Percy. Mind you, if I'm honest, I'd rather be on the beat than standing around here. Still, I suppose you'd say the same, eh?'

'Yeah, we'd all rather be working,' Percy replied, although he wasn't sure that was true. He was having the time of his life organising the pickets, and the idea of going back to fighting for a shift at the dock gate and hefting cargo around didn't appeal, even if getting paid for it did. 'Mind you, I think the ne'er-do-wells are enjoying having you coppers all tied up with the strike. While you lot have been hanging around the picket lines, there have been a couple of break-ins around here.'

'Tell me about it.' Charlie shook his head sadly. 'There was another one last night. They tried to get into a jeweller's shop on East

Street. Mr Emanuel's no fool, though. He leaves his dog loose in the shop at night. A great big bullmastiff it is. The villains got more than they bargained for, and no mistake.'

The image of the crooks coming face to face with a huge, salivating dog made both men chuckle.

'That's almost as funny as the strikers in Plymouth beating the police in a football match the other day.' Percy wiped his eyes. 'Maybe we should organise something similar here? I'd put my money on the dockers.'

The conversation was cut short when one of the young blackleg lads came tearing out of the dock gate in an obvious state of distress.

'Get help!' He stopped in front of the constables, put his hands on his knees and gasped for breath. 'There's been an accident – the crane – two men are trapped. I think one is dead.'

He was only a young lad, probably sixteen or seventeen, with dark brows that didn't match his fair hair. He couldn't seem to catch his breath and was fighting back tears.

Charlie immediately dashed off, presumably to summon an ambulance, and Percy did his best to calm the boy and get more information. The other pickets looked on with interest but made no move to help. Percy was livid when he heard Jimmy mutter, 'Serves the buggers right.'

Luckily for Jimmy, he was too concerned with the frightened lad to respond. 'What's your name?' he asked, more to soothe him than from any real interest.

'Walter.' The boy was still gasping and so pale it looked as if he might collapse.

'Well then, Walter, or should I call you Wally?' Percy gently sat him against the wall of the post office building before he fell. 'I had a mate called Wally in France. A fine chap he was, ended up as a sergeant, I think. Now, just take some deep breaths and calm yourself down.'

*

By the time the ambulance rattled to a halt at the dock gate, Percy had a good idea what had happened and where, but Walter was still in a pitiful state. He left him in the care of one of the constables and went to the cab of the ambulance to speak to the driver, a large man with a huge, angular, almost bovine face.

'Sounds like you've got two casualties,' he said. 'One is crushed, and the other is possibly dead. I'm pretty sure I know where they are. Do you want me to show you?'

'Jump in.'

Percy ran round to the opposite side of the ambulance. He was surprised to see a second man sitting beside the driver. He was much smaller, with wispy grey hair, a snub nose and little dark eyes like currants in a bun. The man slid along the seat to make room, but Percy didn't get in. The pickets had formed an angry blockade in front of the vehicle. Jimmy and Arthur were at the forefront, egging them on. No surprises there.

'Unless he's got a permit, he's not getting past,' Arthur shouted. He scowled, pulled a thick wooden cosh from the inner pocket of his jacket and began to strike it menacingly into his uninjured hand.

'Let the blackleg buggers die,' Jimmy growled.

'What the fuck is wrong with you?' Percy pushed his shoulders back and walked towards them with his fists clenched ready for a fight. 'There are men in there injured. It's a strike, not a war. Even in the war, we might have shot the bloody Hun and blown them up, but we didn't leave wounded men to die without help. Now move out of the way or you'll have me to answer to, and you know dammed well you wouldn't like that!'

By this time, the two remaining constables had joined Percy. They drew their truncheons and stood, rather nervously he thought, facing the pickets. Arthur sulkily put his cosh back into his jacket and Jimmy glowered, but, like the rest of the pickets, moved aside. Percy climbed into the ambulance beside the beady-eyed man and waited for the constables to open the gates. The smell, a combination of petrol, oil and some kind of disinfectant, evoked a vivid memory of being loaded into the back of a similar ambulance on the Western Front, with Lenny holding his hand and looking as sick as a dog. He shuddered.

In the time it took for the gates to be pulled open, a young woman appeared. She was a tiny thing dressed in a dark blue coat. Her platinum blonde hair peeked out beneath a matching hat.

'I'm a nurse,' she said. 'I was walking in the park when I saw the ambulance. Perhaps I can help.'

The angry pickets, deprived of their fight, crowded round and began to jostle her. She looked like a frightened rabbit. The men were teetering on the edge of violence.

'For pity's sake,' Percy muttered under his breath. Then he reached out, grabbed her tiny hand and hauled her into the ambulance beside him.

*

In his time working at the docks, Percy had seen plenty of accidents, but the sight that greeted them at the dockside was not one he wished to ever see again. A pile of sugar sacks, each weighing upwards of two hundredweight, had fallen from the sling. The idiot blacklegs obviously hadn't loaded it properly. What on earth were they thinking by using the cranes without knowing what they were doing? One man lay flat on his back, his sightless eyes staring at the sky. Blood was puddled around his crushed skull. One of the fallen bags had split, and a small drift of spilled sugar was slowly soaking up the gore. There was no helping him, so Percy immediately turned towards the second victim. He was pale and groaning. Several of the fallen sacks had trapped one of his legs.

The other blacklegs were standing around the crane from which the sacks had fallen with horrified looks on their faces, like turkeys waiting for Christmas. Not one of them had thought to try and move the sacks or comfort the man in any way. With a sigh, Percy leapt into action. Between him and the two ambulance men, the sacks were soon moved. One look at the crushed leg was enough to tell Percy it was serious. It was bent at a peculiar angle and blood was seeping through the fabric of the lad's trousers. A cold shiver of recognition ran up Percy's spine as he recalled the injury to his own leg, and his thighbone sticking through the rip in his trousers.

While the two ambulance men covered the other victim and transferred him to their vehicle, the young nurse set to work on the crushed leg. Percy didn't much want to look; his wounds might have healed, but the memory was still raw, so he cradled the man's head and began to speak quietly to him.

'I'm Percy. What's your name, mate?'

'Horace.'

He was just a kid, with sandy curls and a peach fuzz moustache.

'Well, Horace, don't you worry. The nurse here will patch you up in a jiffy.' He wasn't at all sure this was true. The lad's skin was cold and clammy, and his teeth were chattering. The fact he wasn't screaming in pain spoke volumes. Percy had seen enough wounded men to know the quiet ones were the ones to worry about. 'It'll feel better once she's got you bandaged up and in that ambulance.'

'Is it bad?' Horace tried to sit up.

'Can you keep him still?' The nurse looked up from her work.

To avoid looking at the bloody mess that had once been Horace's leg, Percy focused on her big blue eyes. They matched the powder blue dress she wore beneath her coat. The thin fabric clung to her small, pert breasts. He struggled for a moment to tear his eyes away from her.

'Just relax here with me and stay still.' Percy put his hands on Horace's shoulders and gently pulled him back down. 'It's better not to look, believe me. I wish I hadn't when I got blown up in France. These things always look far worse than they are, but the image sticks in your head.'

'Is it bad, though?' Horace's frightened eyes stared into Percy's.

'Not nearly as bad as mine was, mate, and I'm still running around, aren't I.' This was another lie. From what he'd seen, the lad's leg was nothing but mincemeat, but it was better he didn't know that.

'I'm supposed to have a cricket match next week.' His breath was ragged now, rapid and shallow. Percy could almost smell his fear.

'I think you'll have to sit that one out, mate. Give someone else a chance.' The words made him think of when he'd asked Joe about the wound stripes. Now he knew what it was like on the other side of the fence.

'But I'm their best batter.'

'And I was the best damned shot in the whole British infantry, but I had to sit out the rest of the war. It's the way it goes, Horace. It seems like the end of the world at the time, but it really isn't, I promise you. There's more to life than war and cricket.' Somehow, he managed to make it sound like the truth.

'If I couldn't play cricket again . . .'

Tears were welling in Horace's eyes. They reminded Percy of his own bitter tears when Joe told him his war was over.

'I know what you're saying.' He squeezed the lad's shoulders. 'The army was my whole life. I had big plans. One day, I was going to be a sergeant, or maybe even an officer. The shell that got me put paid to all that, but you know what, life goes on. Things don't always turn out how you planned, but you pick yourself up, carry on and make a new life. Who knows, it might turn out better than you ever thought.'

Finally, the nurse had done what she could and, while the ambulance men got poor Horace onto a stretcher and prepared to move him, she turned to Percy. She had blood on her thin summer dress and her hat was askew. He wanted to reach up and straighten it, but that would have been presumptuous, so he restrained himself.

'Thank you for all your help there.' She smiled up at him. Her lashes were surprisingly dark and long for someone so fair. 'That was some story you told him. Was it true?'

'Mostly,' Percy grinned. 'At least the part about being blown up. I'm not sure I was really the best shot in the infantry.'

'You disappoint me.' She looked at him through those long lashes with a half-smile. Her teeth were small and very white. 'I thought I was talking to a real-life hero.'

'No, just a stupid infantryman who got too close to a shell,' he winked.

'Well, thank you again.' She turned to go back to the ambulance.

'What's your name?' he called after her.

'Winnie Monk,' she called back.

19 - Tuesday 11 May 1926

Laura took the iron off the range, spat on it to test the temperature, then carefully began to smooth out the creases in the last of the shirts from her pile of laundry. Her stomach rumbled. She hadn't had any breakfast. There was no telling how long the strike was going to last, so she was doing her best to make the food they had stretch and keep as much money back as possible. Of everyone in the house, she was the one who needed feeding the least, even if her noisy stomach protested.

She glanced over at Lenny, who was sitting at the rickety old kitchen table with his sketchbook balanced on his knee. When they first met, he was always drawing, but with work and the children, he rarely had the time these days. He looked at her and smiled. She might be imagining it, but his face seemed a little less gaunt, and he certainly wasn't coughing as much. The strike, and not having to work all those hours, was doing him good. It couldn't last, of course, nor would she want it to. If he didn't work, they'd starve. She just wished he didn't have to work so hard.

'I'll put the kettle on and make you a cup of tea.' Lenny placed his sketchbook and pencil on the table and crossed the kitchen. 'It looks like you've nearly finished there, and you could do with a sit down. Besides, Percy will probably be back soon. He was only supposed to be checking on the pickets. I hope there haven't been any more accidents or any trouble.'

'Do you think he's all right? He's been a bit odd since he came back yesterday.' She folded the shirt and put it on the pile of clean clothes in the basket on the table. As she did so, she glanced at Lenny's sketch. It was of her. He'd perfectly captured the way her hair curled as it hung across her cheek, the straight line of her nose and the dark curve of her brows. The face on the paper was far more beautiful than the one she saw in the mirror, though. Was that how he saw her?

'I think seeing that chap with his leg crushed affected him.' Lenny got two cups out of the cabinet and put them on the table. 'It was probably a bit close to home. He said the lad was crying because he thought he'd never be able to play cricket again.'

'I don't suppose seeing the other man with his head bashed in helped much, either.' She sank down onto the nearest chair gratefully. Her feet hurt and her head was beginning to ache. She could see how the accident at the docks might have upset Percy, but there was something else going on, too. There'd been a change in him since yesterday, a subtle softening. If she didn't know better, she'd have said there was a woman behind it. But unless there were women hanging round the picket line, he hadn't been anywhere lately to meet one.

'At least there wasn't any trouble, even if it was touch and go when the ambulance arrived.' Lenny spooned tea into the pot. 'Percy was furious with Arthur and Jimmy about that. I wouldn't want to be in their shoes today.'

'There's been plenty of trouble elsewhere, though. Hetty Porter told me there's been violence all over the country. Pickets throwing stuff at the O.M.S. lot driving trams and buses. A huge mob, in London I think, knocked a wall down and used all the bricks to throw, or so she said.'

'How does she know that? It sounds more like propaganda to me, just like during the war. She's a bit of a gossip from what I hear. I wouldn't believe everything she tells you.'

The kettle began to whistle, and Lenny took it off the hob.

'The Porters have a radio. She heard it on the BBC, so it must be true. They're broadcasting news every day. She said a member of the British Fascists deliberately drove his van into a crowd of demonstrators in London. A man was seriously hurt, and the crowd turned on the driver, dragged him out of the van and almost lynched him.'

Percy walked through the door. 'That's the best bloody thing to do with fascists. I hope there's enough tea in that pot for me. I'm gasping.'

20 - Wednesday 12 May 1926

It was almost time for the evening pickets to arrive. The blue sky had clouded over but Lenny hadn't noticed. He and Percy were leaning against the post office wall beside the dock gate engaged in a heated conversation with Charlie West about the derailing of the Flying Scotsman.

'It was being driven by scabs, though.' Percy scowled. 'Everyone on board was aware of the danger. They've been stoning the trains ever since the blacklegs started running them. I heard the miners' wives ran down to the tracks with bandages but got told to, "Get back to their dirty pit villages" by the people from the train.'

'I'm not saying I don't have sympathy with the miners, but it wasn't right for them to take up the rails like they did.' Charlie puffed out his cheeks. 'Imagine if people had been killed. It was only luck there weren't hundreds of dead. Then we'd have goodness knows how many miners going to the gallows. There's a line, and those miners crossed it.'

'He's right.' Lenny knew Percy wouldn't like it, but he had to agree with Charlie. 'There was really no excuse for taking such a stupid risk. There were five hundred people on that train. Just think about what could have happened. More to the point, think about how the public would have reacted. If the miners want to win this, they need the public on their side. Do you think they'll ever catch the men who did it, Charlie?'

'Maybe, maybe not,' Charlie said with a tight-lipped smile. 'No one's talking, but I have a feeling the police up there in Cramlington have a good idea who's responsible. Proving it is another matter.'

A few spots of rain had just begun to fall. Percy had opened his mouth to say something else when Harry Smith strolled around the corner of the post office building. His collar was turned up and his hat was pulled down over his eyes, almost as if he didn't want to be recognised. Of course, Harry liked to keep a low profile. Percy nudged Lenny and nodded in Harry's direction.

With his hands in his pockets and his head down, Harry walked to the front of the group of pickets chatting at the dock gate. He stood for a moment then clapped his hands and said, 'Listen up. I've got an announcement.' He didn't have to say it twice. He had everyone's attention. Even the constables moved forward and listened intently.

'I have a message from the TUC here.' He pulled a piece of paper from his pocket, unfolded it and began to read. 'The General Strike has ended. It has not failed. It has secured the resumption of the negotiations in the coal industry, and the continuance, during negotiations, of the financial assistance given by the government—'

Harry's speech was interrupted by a growing babble from the pickets.

'But the second line, the shipbuilders and engineers, have only just come out,' Dan Painter shouted.

'Does this mean we've won?' Tommy Munn called out.

'Does this mean we go back to work tomorrow?' Albie Joyce scratched his head.

Everyone was talking at once. No one knew what to make of it. There were frowns, confused faces and shaking heads all round.

When the hubbub finally died down, Harry continued. 'Comrades, we have done what we set out to do. We've shown the mine owners and the government that we mean business. The government will support the miners while the talks continue, and our solidarity will have a huge impact on those talks. I'm sure there will soon be a satisfactory conclusion.' He looked again at the paper in his hand. 'The TUC has said we should forget all recrimination, let our employers act with generosity and give our whole hearts loyally to our work. We should put all malice and vindictiveness behind us.'

Lenny wasn't convinced this was the victory Harry seemed to be making it out to be. There was something off about his manner. The way he read from his piece of paper and the stilted words. If they'd really won, why wasn't he cheering and talking about victory? There was something fishy about it, but whatever had really happened, the end of the strike was good news for him and Laura.

'Bugger all this talk.' Percy smiled as if he really did think they'd won. 'Let's go to the pub and celebrate.'

21 - Friday 14 May 1926

Laura staggered into the hallway. Water dripped from the ends of her hair and her feet sloshed in her boots. The street outside was like a river, and the rain continued to come down in sheets. If this kept up much longer, it'd be over the doorsill and inside the house. She took off her dripping coat and hung it on the newel post before plonking her soggy hat on top of it. The coat was wool, and the hat was felt; both would take forever to dry out. She could hear the steady drip of rain falling into the bucket on the upstairs landing. She'd have to empty it soon, before it overflowed. At this rate, she'd have to take the tin bath up there; a bucket wasn't going to last out the night. She left her wet boots at the bottom of the stairs and walked barefoot into the kitchen, still fuming over her encounter with her landlord, Mr Miller. She'd trudged more than two miles in the pouring rain to ask him to fix the hole in the roof. How many times would she have to ask before he did something about it?

'I can't get anyone up on the roof when it's raining like this.' He'd shrugged his narrow shoulders.

'Well, then, I can't pay the rent while the rain is dripping through my bloody roof,' she'd snapped.

He'd stared at her with his piggy eyes, as if she were something nasty he'd stepped in. She wanted to slap his pink, porcine face. Then, without another word, he turned, went back inside his warm, dry house and shut the door on her. It was all right for him. His roof wasn't leaking, and his walls weren't black with mould. He was happy enough to take their money every week, though.

She put the kettle on the stove, pulled one of the chairs out from the kitchen table and sat down with a sigh. The rain hammered at the grimy little kitchen window. She put her elbows on the table and rubbed her temples. Was Lenny inside in the dry or out standing on the dock? She worried about him getting soaked all day, but at least it wasn't cold, and she supposed she should be grateful he'd been able to go straight back to work. It was more than could be said for Percy. Along with Arthur Fisk, Jimmy Pothecary and several of the other pickets, he'd been marked down as an agitator and turned away at the dock gate, just as she'd known he would be. He'd come home defeated, as if all the sense of purpose and pride he'd had during the strike had evaporated. If he ever got a shift again, he'd have to consider himself lucky.

Just as the kettle began to whistle, Percy came through the door. 'It's raining cats and dogs out there.' He took off his cap and put it on the kitchen table. Water immediately began to puddle around it.

'I did notice.' She pointed to her own wet hair and shoulders.

'What were you doing out in it?'

'I went to see Miller about mending the hole in the roof. In case you hadn't spotted it, there's water pouring in again.'

With a heavy sigh and a dirty look, she picked up Percy's cap and hung it on the hook on the back door. Then she started mopping up the water with a tea towel.

'Oh, and there was me thinking that bucket was just for decoration.' He curled his top lip. 'You might have saved yourself a journey. Pigs will fly before that bugger fixes the roof.'

'Well, I had to try, didn't I? Talking of trying, I suppose you got turned away again this morning? Where have you been since then? In the pub drowning your sorrows with your communist friends?'

'Actually, there was no point going to the docks at all. It's clear they're not going to take us back, despite what Harry said. Jimmy heard they were taking on warehouse men at May and Wade, so we went down there instead.'

'And did you get anything?' Laura raised her eyebrows. At least he was being realistic and seriously looking for work outside the docks.

'Only wet.' He shook his head angrily. 'Five jobs there were, and fifty men or more waiting in line for them in the pouring rain. It was almost as bad as standing in the scrum at the dock gate waiting to be picked, except there wasn't any fighting.'

'Well, you might as well make the tea while I go and get my knitting. The sooner I get Mrs Wilson's christening shawl finished the sooner I get paid. One of us has to earn some money. While you're at it, you could empty that bloody bucket, too. Take the tin bath up to put under the leak.'

'Yes, sir.' He clicked his heels and saluted her.

She poked out her tongue and went to the parlour to collect her knitting.

The knitting bag was on the floor by the front window next to the sewing machine. As she bent to pick it up, she noticed a man slowly walking down the street. He appeared to be looking at the house numbers. The rain on the window made it difficult to see clearly, but he was wearing a long, dark coat and a fedora hat. She crouched down below the windowsill out of sight. Had Mr Miller sent him because she'd said she wasn't going to pay the rent? It wouldn't be the first time she'd hidden when the rent man came, and it probably wouldn't be the last. This man wasn't the normal rent man, but he certainly looked sinister. She stayed hidden for several minutes. Hopefully, Percy wouldn't be stupid enough to open the door if he knocked. Then, when she finally judged the danger to be over, she cautiously lifted her head and peered through the bottom of the window. The man had gone past her door, but he was still out there. Whoever he was, he looked like bad news for someone.

'What took you so long?' Percy said when she went back into the kitchen.

Before she had the chance to reply, Sally Hopgood burst

through the back door like a tiny tornado wrapped in wet rags.

'I hope you don't mind me climbing over the wall and coming through your yard, but I think the tallyman is outside.' She brushed a strand of sodden black hair off her face. 'Can I hide in here a minute? I meant to pawn Bill's Sunday suit this morning, but I didn't want to go out in this rain.'

'I saw a man out there just now. I thought he might be a new rent collector,' replied Laura. 'I almost climbed over the back wall myself and went to hide in your house,' she added with a chuckle.

Sally was a good neighbour. She was always willing to share what she had. Her two boys, Eddie and Ernie, played with Bobby and Gladys and went to the picture house with them on Saturday mornings.

'Lately, I seem to spend half my life hiding from people who want money I don't have.' Sally shook her head and took a seat at the kitchen table. 'This one looked a right brute, too. He had a face like a bloody monkey, with great big ginger whiskers.'

'Are you sure he was the tallyman?' Percy frowned. 'Did he actually knock on your door?'

'I don't know. I didn't stay around long enough to find out,' Sally replied.

Why Percy looked so concerned about the tallyman was a mystery. Of all the things they did have to worry about, paying back borrowed money wasn't one of them. Mum and Dad didn't hold with getting things on tick and neither of them had ever borrowed a penny in their lives.

22 - Wednesday 19 May 1926

Hidden in the shadows of the alley beside the workhouse school, Percy stared across the road at the long, narrow windows of the old workhouse building. At this rate, he'd soon be looking at them from the inside. He'd searched for work everywhere, but all he'd found were masses of other men doing the same. He'd even been back to the dock gate a couple of times, but he might as well have been invisible. Harry Smith had played him. He could see that now. All his talk about revolution, and his guarantee there'd be no victimisation was hot air. None of the main players amongst the pickets had worked since the strike ended. It was all right for Harry; the union looked after him. While Percy was controlling the pickets every day, Harry was nowhere to be seen. Now, though, it was Harry who took all the credit for the lack of violence.

A black cat scurried across the road and disappeared over the school wall. In the fifteen minutes he'd been lurking in the darkness leaning against the damp bricks, it was the only living creature he'd seen. It was well past midnight, and all the decent people were in bed. One way or another, he'd been hiding all day.

This morning, when he overheard the conversation that led him here, he'd been skulking behind a pillar in the quietest corner of the Bell and Crown, bitterly nursing a glass with about an inch of beer at the bottom of it. He'd been hiding from Amy and her sharp tongue. She'd made it clear she was fed up with him sitting in the pub half the day without actually buying a drink.

'Much as I love you, Percy Barfoot, this is a pub not a bloody waiting room.'

Trouble was he had no money for more than one drink, and he certainly didn't want to go home to Laura and all her 'I told you so' looks.

Now he was hiding from Arthur Fisk, Jimmy Pothecary and Sam Strange, or at least waiting for them. He hadn't intended to eavesdrop on their conversation. Truth to tell, he'd only caught the last part of it as they left the bar, but he distinctly heard Arthur say, 'Right then, lads, I'll see you at half past midnight outside St Mary's. Don't be late. And Sam, make sure you don't forget anything this time.' They were obviously up to something. He was certain they were the ones who broke into George Jones's shop. If they were planning another robbery, this might be his chance to get some proof.

When he heard the murmur of voices, he knew it must be them. Who else would be out at this time of night? The sound of Arthur's big gob confirmed it. Percy shrank further along the alley. If they spotted him, he'd be hard pushed to explain what he was up to. Right now, they weren't exactly his biggest fans. They'd all believed Harry's rubbish about the revolution. They thought the strike would have been won if they'd had their way and cracked a few heads, and they blamed him for not letting them. Once they'd walked past, he poked his head around the corner of the wall. They were heading up towards the market square. He waited until they'd disappeared around the slight bend in the road before following.

Warily, he stuck to the shadows and ducked from one shop doorway to the next. They passed the empty market square without looking back. The road ahead was straight now, but once he got past the deserted market there were side streets to duck down. He didn't want to lose them, but nor did he want to be seen. When they reached Six Dials, he shimmied around the corner of Craven Street and flattened himself against the wall. He could hear his heart thumping in his chest. If only he had a periscope like they'd had in the trenches, he'd be able to see which direction they'd turned. Cautiously, he poked his head around the corner. They'd disappeared over the slight hump of the railway bridge. With six roads converging at the junction ahead, he couldn't afford to wait any longer or they'd have disappeared altogether.

He ran up to the Six Dials junction. For a moment, he thought he'd left it too long and lost them. He looked right, towards the gasometers. The street was empty. Unless they'd started running, they hadn't gone up towards the town, either. With his heart sinking, he crossed the wide expanse of road. He felt exposed out in the open, as if he was in No Man's Land. Then, with a sigh of relief, he spotted them some way along St Mary's Road. He pressed against the wall on the corner and waited until they were as far as the bend beyond the school before making a move. So far, they hadn't looked back once, but the terraced houses here, with their front steps and railings around basement windows, wouldn't provide much cover if they did. As soon as they were out of sight, he dashed along the street. He turned the bend in time to see them approaching the next big junction. There were now only three possible directions they could go, but he could still easily lose them if he missed which road they took.

This was the moment he almost came unstuck. He was so intent on seeing which way they went that he kept creeping forwards, closing the distance. They'd stopped dead in their tracks, seemingly to have a whispered conversation. When Sam nervously began to turn his head this way and that, as if checking they weren't being watched, Percy dashed down the nearest side road. He was sure he hadn't been spotted, but it wasn't worth taking any chances. He was almost certain they were going towards Onslow Road. Of the three alternatives, it was the one with the most businesses and shops. He could see the hospital to his left, which was all windows and chimneys in the dark. If he ran around the perimeter, he could come out behind them again without being seen.

He ran as fast as he could; left onto Exmoor Road then left again onto Fanshawe Street. He spotted the chapel, with its ornate arched window and the four little towers at the corners, and was so busy thinking about where the men could have got to that he failed to look where he was going. By the time he saw the slight figure in the gloom, it was too late to avoid clattering into it. The diminutive size and the dark cape told him it was a nurse. There was no time to swerve, but somehow, he managed to slow down enough to catch her in his arms rather than knock her over.

'I'm so sorry.' With great embarrassment, he released her from his grip and stepped back to a more respectable distance.

'You should watch where you're going, running about in the dark like that.' The nurse straightened her skirts and cape crossly.

As she turned, he caught sight of her face in the glow of a streetlamp. It was Winnie Monk, the nurse who'd looked after the injured man at the docks. She must have recognised him at almost the same moment. Her pretty face broke into a smile. 'Oh, it's you. Percy, wasn't it, the stupid infantryman? What on earth are you doing here in the middle of the night?'

'Testing out a theory.' He grinned and looked at her. The cape hid those perky little breasts, and, in the darkness, the startling blue of her eyes wasn't as noticeable, but those long, dark lashes made his heart flutter. Suddenly, he didn't care at all what Fisk and his cronies were up to, or where they were going. 'What about you?'

'I work here.' She arched her eyebrows. 'I'm a nurse, remember?'

'How could I forget such a beautiful face? But isn't it a bit late for you to be wandering around the streets on your own?'

'Well, it's the only way I've found so far to get from work to home at the end of my shift. If you can think of a better one, I should like to know it. Besides, I only live on Northumberland Road; it isn't far.'

'As it happens, I was going that way myself.' It was a lie, although it was in the general direction of home. 'The least I could do is walk with you and make sure you get back safely.'

'What, in case there are any more mad infantrymen running around trying to knock me down?' She teased him, but she took the arm he offered all the same.

They walked through the quiet streets, past terraced houses with dark windows. She talked a lot, but he was happy to listen. She told him how she liked the late shift because it gave her time during the day to wander in the parks and enjoy the sunshine. She said she'd been born in London and was an only child. Although Percy could cheerfully strangle Laura when she got on his back, he couldn't imagine life without her, Willy, Ethel, Maria or Lizzie. He felt sorry for Winnie to have missed out on all the shared memories and experiences that come with siblings. She told him she'd lived in London until she was ten, when her father got a job with White Star as a steward.

'He almost ended up on the Titanic. His cousin William went down with her. He says he had a bad feeling about that ship all along. Seamen are very superstitious, you know.'

When they turned onto Northumberland Road, she finally seemed to run out of things to talk about. So far, Percy had hardly said a word. His chance to make a good impression was fast disappearing, but the only thing he could think to say was, 'Do you know what happened to Horace, that poor lad who got his leg crushed at the docks?'

Her face clouded over. 'Actually, I do. I went to see him the next day. His leg couldn't be saved. It was crushed too badly and for too long. He was distraught. He kept talking about not being able to play cricket again and life not being worth living, so I reminded him of the things you'd said to him at the dockside. "If a man like Percy – who has been to war to fight for his country and witnessed all manner of horrors – can get over his injuries," I said, "a young man like you, with an education and a wealthy family, should be able to." Then I told him about some of the young men I saw in France and on the hospital ships. Men with no limbs, no faces and their minds destroyed by what they saw. I said he should count himself lucky he'd missed out on all of that. I'm not sure if it will make any difference, of course, but it's true.'

Poor Horace. Percy knew exactly how he must be feeling. Still, one man's disaster was often another man's good luck, and from where he was standing, bumping into Winnie again certainly seemed like good luck.

23 - Sunday 23 May 1926

Sunday was the best day of the week. No getting up early for work, a lovely dinner and family all around the table. Lenny smiled at the plates piled with roast potatoes, carrots, peas, young marrow and spring greens – all from Laura's Dad's garden – not to mention slices of juicy pork belly with crispy crackling. You couldn't beat a bit of crackling, some sweet applesauce and lashings of rich, thick gravy.

'This is a lovely bit of pork, Laura.' He smiled across the table at her.

'It was the last bit in the shop.' She speared a piece of carrot with her fork and smiled back. 'Mr Robinson let me have it cheap. You get the best bargains by going in on Saturday afternoon, just before closing time. He said his family always have whatever's left that won't keep until Monday.'

'If it's good enough for him, it's good enough for us, eh?' He took a slice of bread from the plate in the middle of the table to mop up his gravy.

'It's a pity Amy Medway doesn't sell off her stock at the weekend, too,' Percy said through a mouthful of pork. 'Now, wouldn't that be a thing?'

'We'd never get you out of the pub,' Laura sniggered. 'Gladys, leave some bread for Bobby. Honestly, I swear you've got hollow legs like your father.'

Lenny smiled fondly at his daughter as she stuffed gravy-soaked bread into her face. He had no idea where she put it all, but she could certainly eat for England. He wondered if her namesake would have been the same had she lived. His memories of his little sister were quite hazy now. He'd only been fourteen when she died. It wasn't long after they'd moved to the big house on the other side of the river, and he always associated her death with the change, just as he associated Jesse's death with the coal dust from the gasworks. He looked at Bobby, with his mouth full of roast potato and gravy on his chin, and then at the peeling wallpaper and green-black mould on the walls. His children deserved more than this. With the strike over, maybe he could start looking for better places to rent. Somewhere on the other side of the river would be nice, although it would make getting to work difficult. Perhaps he could get a bicycle. Who was he kidding? He could never afford a bicycle.

'He'd be better off getting a dog, like old man Emanuel. Don't you think, Len?' Percy stared at him.

What was he talking about? 'Sorry, Percy, I was daydreaming.' Lenny smiled, as a vision of riding to work on a huge dog sprang into his head.

'I said, George Jones was so worried about the burglars coming back that he's taken to sleeping in the shop. I told him he'd be better off getting a dog, like old man Emanuel in East Street.'

Lenny's mind snapped back to the present. 'The way it's going, every shopkeeper in the town will be getting dogs,' he said. 'Apparently, the newsagents on Onslow Road got robbed on Wednesday night.'

'Petheridges?' Percy paused with his fork halfway to his mouth.

'That's the one.'

'Where did you hear about that?'

'Tommy Munn told me yesterday. His mother lives a few doors down from the shop. Mr Petheridge disturbed them at it. He said there were two of them, big chaps by all accounts, with scarves tied around their faces. He got badly beaten. Tommy says he's lucky to be alive. They got away with loads of tobacco and a little bit of money.'

'That's terrible, but it's not talk for the dinner table, or little ears.' Laura gave Lenny a dirty look then took a slice of bread and began to mop her plate.

'I saw a burglar the other day.' Gladys eyed the last slice of bread greedily. 'He was walking down our road looking at all the houses.'

'Don't be silly. No one round here's got anything worth stealing.' Laura's dirty look turned into one of her 'I told you so' stares.

'What did this burglar look like?' Percy put his knife and fork down with a frown and bit his bottom lip.

Surely, he didn't believe Gladys had really seen a burglar. Laura was right; no one round here had anything worth taking. Gladys probably didn't even know what a burglar was. No doubt she was making up a tale to get attention. It was likely just a tradesman of some kind, or her imagination. She was a great one for stories.

'He was a posh man, with a long black coat, a big scarf and a funny hat.' She arched her hands above her head, mimicking a trilby or maybe a homburg. 'It was just after you came home from the Bell and Crown, Uncle Percy, when me and Bobby was playing football. You found some blackjacks behind our ears. They turned my tongue black, remember? Bobby saw him, too, didn't you, Bobby?'

'Yeah. He was looking in all the windows,' Bobby said matter-of-factly, before taking the opportunity to grab the bread, much to Gladys's disgust. She folded her arms and pouted.

'Did he have big side whiskers?' Percy pointed to the sides of his face.

'No, he had a big fat moustache, like a furry caterpillar on his lip.' Gladys stuck her finger across her top lip and waggled it. 'And he had very shiny shoes.'

'That wasn't a burglar, Gladys,' Laura said. 'It was probably the new tallyman. I saw him the other day, too. I expect lots of people have borrowed money because of the strike. I suppose he's the closest thing to a burglar we're ever going to have around here, though.'

Lenny wondered why Percy looked so worried about Gladys's silly story. Surely, he hadn't borrowed money or got something on the never-never? He'd looked worried about the break in at Petheridges, too. Laura was right, there was something going on with him, and Lenny had an idea it had to do with Fisk. Even Percy wouldn't be daft enough to get involved in crime, though, would he?

24 - Saturday 29 May 1926

Someone was throwing pebbles at the bedroom window. Laura opened her eyes. It was too dark to make out anything other than vague shapes of light and shade. The sound came again. With a sigh of relief, she realised it was just the wind throwing rain against the glass. She turned over, snuggled into Lenny's warmth and listened to the rhythmic sound of his breathing. Unlike her, nothing seemed to rouse him. It must be all the practice he'd had sleeping through shells and whatnot in France. Another gust of wind threw yet more rain against the window and Laura slowly became aware of another sound, a dull tap-tap-tapping out in the hallway. It took a few moments for her brain to wake up enough to work out it was water dripping through the roof. Mr Miller still hadn't got anyone round to fix the leak, even though she'd relented and paid the rent. She cursed him under her breath and slid out of bed as quietly as she could.

Shivering a little, she crept downstairs. By the temperature, you'd never know it was nearly June. She stumbled about in the dark in her nightdress, stubbing her toe on the leg of the kitchen table as she reached under it for the bucket and stifling a yelp. If she'd put the light on, she might have saved herself the pain, but then she'd never have been able to get back to sleep. Mr Miller had a lot to answer for. In the morning, she'd ask Percy to go up into the attic and see if he could patch the hole up somehow. It wasn't as if he had anything better to do these days. To be fair, he was trying hard to find work.

Since the strike, so many other men were doing the same; it was like finding a needle in a haystack. His scar didn't help. It made him look like a thug and put people off. The dole money was such a paltry sum, he'd have starved if it wasn't for her and Lenny. So much for a land fit for heroes.

Back upstairs, with the bucket now catching the rain, she burrowed under the covers and shut her eyes. Lenny was snoring so she poked at his leg with her cold toe. He snuffled, snorted and rolled over, still sound asleep. At least he stopped snoring. The rain carried on lashing against the window, and now there was a metallic drip-drip-drip of water falling into the bucket. She began to fantasise about all the ways she could get revenge on Mr Miller. It was better than counting sheep. Little by little, she relaxed, warmed up and began to drift back to sleep. The sounds of rain against the window and rain dropping into the bucket began to fade away. Then, suddenly, she was wide-awake again, staring into the darkness. What was that sound? It was almost like a key turning in a lock. Was someone trying to break in? Unlikely as it seemed, had Gladys been right about seeing a burglar? She held her breath and strained her ears. Someone was trying to get in the front door!

Gradually, she let out her breath. Silence. Gladys and her silly story about burglars had got her imagining things now. She tried to relax her tense muscles. Then there was a long slow creak and, a few seconds later, a definite click. Someone really had come in the front door. Fear tingled through her body like a bolt of electricity. She thought about waking Lenny. Then she remembered the newsagent on Onslow Road. She'd rather they took what little they could find than risk Lenny or Percy getting hurt.

If there really were burglars, they'd picked the wrong house. She stayed still and stiff, listening. What if they found the emergency tin? It may have looked like an ordinary cocoa tin pushed to the back of the cupboard, but every penny she'd saved was in there. A burglar was hardly going to make himself a hot drink in the middle of robbing a house, though. She could hear her own heart beating. The squeaky stair creaked. The burglar was coming upstairs! Now she could hardly breathe for fear, and her heart was so loud she was sure the intruder would be able to hear it. She almost jumped out of her skin when a clatter announced they had kicked the bucket on the landing. This was followed by a whispered curse. It was Percy's voice. What the hell was he doing out at this time of night? At ten o'clock, when she and Lenny went to bed, he'd been reading the paper and had just lit a cigarette. She thought she'd heard him come upstairs to bed a little while later. Why would he go out in the middle of the night?

It took her a long, long time to get back to sleep. All the reasons Percy might have gone out whirled around in her head. None of them were good. She'd put his strange behaviour over the last week or two down to his fruitless search for a job. If it were that, though, she'd have expected him to go into one of his melancholies, but he'd been strangely happy, almost excited.

Now she couldn't stop thinking about all the burglaries. It was unthinkable that Percy could be involved, except, if she'd just thought it, it obviously wasn't unthinkable. After all, he'd been mixed up with Fisk and his gang when they were thieving from the docks, and he hadn't had any work of any kind since the strike. Surely, he wasn't that desperate or stupid?

The other possibility was the Bolsheviks, although Percy swore he was done with them. He was angry with Harry Smith for making out he'd been the one keeping the picket line peaceful instead of giving Percy his due credit. Percy believed Harry had used him and betrayed the dockers, just as the unions had betrayed the miners. Sally said some of the dockers who'd been blacklisted were muttering about another strike, although how they thought they could strike if they were blacklisted was a mystery. Maybe he was getting himself mixed up in that. She sighed and rubbed her eyes. Was she doomed to spend the rest of her life worrying about her stupid brother?

25 - Saturday 29 May 1926

The rain that had soaked Percy on his way back home in the early hours had dried up, just as he'd hoped it would. He turned left at Six Dials and walked towards the parks with a spring in his step. Even Laura's bad mood this morning couldn't dampen his spirits. She'd given him a filthy stare as she slammed his breakfast down in front of him and had barely said a single word to him between then and when he left the house. She must have heard him come in last night when he kicked that blasted bucket. If the children hadn't been there, she might have challenged him about it. No doubt she was thinking the worst of him. She always did, though he knew she'd defend him with her life if she had to. He wasn't quite ready to tell her about his nightly adventures. It was all too fragile and new to risk jinxing.

Fisk and his gang seemed unimportant now. He was certain they'd burgled that newsagents and beaten poor Mr Petheridge half to death, even if he had no proof. It put him in mind of what happened to poor old Fred. Maybe they'd done that, too. Or was he making mountains out of molehills, like Laura with the Bolshevik thing? Obviously, he wasn't going to let it go. One way or another, he'd catch them out, but right now, he had bigger fish to fry.

Winnie would be waiting for him by the statue in the centre of East Park, and he wasn't about to let thoughts of Fisk or Fred ruin his mood. For ten days now, she'd filled his mind. Late each night, he sneaked out of the house, went to the hospital and walked her home from her shifts. Those short walks were like beacons of brightness in his miserable life. She was the best thing that had ever happened to him, and he still couldn't believe she'd finally agreed to meet him in daylight. He probably should have bought her some flowers or something, but it was too late now. Besides, he didn't have any money.

He crossed the road and set off along the avenue of trees, bursting with new leaves. He couldn't have been happier, except he'd had a prickling at the back of his neck ever since leaving Six Dials. He had a strange feeling he was being followed. It was likely just his imagination, because when he'd stopped and casually turned around, there'd been no one there. The business of the stranger lurking around their street was making him jumpy, nothing more. The other week, when Sally said the new tallyman had a face like a monkey and big red whiskers, he couldn't help thinking of the fascists in the Bell and Crown. One of them had looked exactly like that, and he'd seen him again in the crowd on the Common during the strike. Men with red whiskers were hardly uncommon, though. Maybe they all looked like monkeys.

He glanced nervously behind him. There was a man in a long black coat turning into the park. Of course there were men in long black coats all over the place. It didn't mean anything, did it? All the same, he quickened his pace. When the statue came into view, he couldn't see Winnie. His heart fell. Perhaps she'd changed her mind and wasn't coming. He turned around to check on the man in the black coat and was relieved to see him turn off to the left, towards Above Bar Street. When he turned back, Winnie had appeared. Laura was right; he really did need to stop being so pessimistic.

She was wearing the dark blue coat and hat he remembered from their first ever meeting at the dock gate. He imagined her breasts beneath it and walked towards her with a big grin on his face. Her hands were on the railings and her attention on Richard Andrews' statue, or rather the arches, pillars and ornate stonework of the plinth. The statue could only be seen properly from a distance. He stopped beside her, and she turned to him and smiled before tilting her head right back to catch a glimpse of Andrews. Her neck was pale and long. He wondered what it would be like to kiss it then slide his hands inside her dress.

'They called him Southampton's Dick Wittington, you know. He came here a pauper, a farm hand turned blacksmith, and, against all the odds, became the most successful coachbuilder in the town. He employed hundreds and hundreds of men.'

'Did he really?' Percy knew the statue was Richard Andrews, but that was about the extent of his knowledge. He didn't care much for history, but Winnie was always talking about the past, and he'd have walked over hot coals to keep standing by her side.

'Yes.' She took his arm and began to walk towards the road. 'He built a huge factory on Above Bar Street, defied the Tories on the Corn Laws and was mayor four times.'

Winnie was still chattering on about Andrews and his good deeds as they crossed the road towards the cenotaph. For someone who wasn't even born in the town, she knew an awful lot about it. He listened in a perfunctory way, happy to have her on his arm and hear her soft, almost musical voice. The man in the black coat he'd thought was following him earlier was in front of the cenotaph. He took no notice of them as they passed and instead peered intently at the inscriptions, as if he was looking for a particular name. Maybe he was. They took the circular path around the statue of Isaac Watts. Winnie began to talk about hymns and books about logic. Percy nodded and looked at the flowers beginning to open in the beds behind the railings. He wished he could have bought her flowers. When they came to an empty bench, they sat down. The day had turned out to be warm and sunny. He let Winnie's voice flow over him, raised his face to the clear blue sky and sighed. Now they were seated she'd let go of his arm, and he missed the warmth of her hand at his elbow. If only he had the money to take her to the tearooms around the corner. Every single day he walked the streets trying to find work, but no one was taking on men, at least not men like him.

'Why the sad look?' She touched his arm.

'I was just wishing I had a job and some money to treat you to a drink and a cake in the tearooms.'

'I'd far rather sit in the park in the sunshine. The parks in town are simply beautiful, especially at this time of year. It would be a shame to be indoors.'

'You deserve to be showered with flowers and gifts, though. If I had a job, you'd hardly be able to move for the flowers in your arms.'

'You'll get one in the end. I'm sure of it. All your perseverance has to pay off eventually.'

'I think I've got the wrong kind of face.' He pointed to his scar. 'They take one look at me and think I'm a wrong'un. I can hardly believe you've agreed to be seen out in daylight with me.'

'Oh, Percy.' She reached up and tenderly stroked the hideous scar. 'I don't care about your face. It's your kind heart I'm interested in. That was the only thing I saw that day in the dockyard. The way you comforted that poor lad, Horace. You were so gentle with him and showed him such compassion, even though he was one of the strike breakers and you were one of the pickets.'

'Kindness and compassion aren't much of an asset when it comes to warehouse work and the like.' Percy could feel the colour rising in his face and the tingle where her fingers had lingered.

'Well, then, maybe you're wasted in that kind of job. I can see you working in the hospital. On Monday, I'll have a word with the sister and see if she knows of any jobs going for orderlies, or maybe ambulance drivers. Do you know how to drive?'

'Of course.' He'd learned to drive in the Territorial Force. They'd talked about sending him off to the Service Corps as a lorry driver, but he'd wanted to be in the thick of the action with a gun in his hand, so he'd joined the Hampshire's as an infantryman instead. Looking back, he'd have been better off if he'd listened to them. Wasn't that the story of his life?

26 - Sunday 6 June 1926

The house was cleaner than Lenny had ever seen it. Laura had spent the whole week scrubbing and polishing everything to within an inch of its life. She'd waxed the floors, polished the table until it shone, beaten all the rugs and washed the curtains. She'd even made Percy go up into the attic to patch the hole in the roof. All this was in honour of Percy's sweetheart's visit. As far as Lenny could see, the clean floors, rugs and furniture merely emphasised the mouldy walls and the shabbiness of everything they owned, but he thought it best not to point this out to Laura. She wasn't usually the houseproud type, which was just as well, seeing as he hadn't provided her with a house to be proud of. Then again, they didn't usually entertain guests.

Laura had got herself in a right old state about the visit, even though her sister Maria thought there must be something wrong with Winnie if she'd reached the ripe old age of twenty-six without getting married, and her Mum said she must need glasses if she was courting Percy. It was hard to see what all the fuss was about, other than the fact Percy had never brought a woman home before. Of course, none of his previous, short-lived dalliances had been with the kind of girls you'd bring home to meet your sister. This one was different, or so Percy said. He'd painted her as something special. He said she was a real beauty, and clever with it, too.

Lenny looked at her across the dining table. She was pretty

enough, in a rather small, scrawny way, but she wasn't his type at all. He'd far rather have a Rubenesque woman like Laura. Apart from being too thin, to his mind she was rather pale and washed out. What she lacked in colour she made up for by talking almost non-stop. Despite his lovestruck smile, even Percy's eyes had glazed over when she started going on about the stone for the medieval walls being brought from the Isle of Wight; though the children had been all ears when she'd told them about the Southampton Plot and how the culprits had been hanged, drawn and quartered outside the Bargate.

'How interesting.' Laura picked up one of the dainty sandwiches she'd made especially for the occasion. She'd been poring over some of the old magazines Hetty Porter regularly passed onto her. Lenny had flicked through one of them; it was full of advertisements for things like 'reducing soap' to wash away fat, fancy hats, cake recipes and stories that all seemed to involve dapper men of means falling in love with poor, working-class girls.

On the back of her reading, Laura had decided they needed to have afternoon tea rather than the thick slices of bread with salty dripping they usually ate on Sunday evenings. Now the table was spread with the best cloth and positively groaning under the weight of fruitcake and silly triangular potted meat sandwiches with the crusts cut off. Laura said the crusts wouldn't go to waste; she was going to make a bread pudding with them, which was a bonus. The cake was moist and slightly cinnamony, but the sandwiches seemed insubstantial.

'This cake is wonderful.' Winnie put the slice of fruitcake she'd been delicately nibbling onto her plate. 'I'm not much of a cook myself. My mother says I could burn water.'

'Uncle Percy eats lots of cake.' Gladys looked Winnie in the eye with all the innocence of youth. 'If you're going to marry him, you'll have to learn to cook.'

Lenny glanced at Percy, who stared down at his plate as if it was suddenly the most interesting thing in the world, while the colour began to rise slowly from his collar to his cheeks.

'Gladys!' Laura gave her a hard stare.

'Perhaps Uncle Percy should learn to cook himself, so he can make cakes for me,' Winnie said with a stilted smile.

'Don't be silly,' Gladys giggled. 'Men don't cook cakes. Uncle Percy can make money and sweets come out of our ears, though.'

When even Gladys couldn't stuff another potted meat sandwich into her mouth and the cake was all gone, Laura began to clear the table.

'Let me help you with that.' Winnie began to pile up the plates nearest to her.

'Nonsense, you're a guest.' Laura motioned for her to sit down. She probably didn't want her to see the kitchen, with its wonky table, mismatched chairs and scuffed old cabinet. No doubt she was also hoping Winnie wouldn't want to use the privy, either, because then she'd have to admit it was at the far end of the yard. If she stuck with Percy, though, she'd have to get used to slum living, because it was all he was ever going to be able to provide.

'It's the least I can do after such a lovely tea. You wash and I'll wipe.'

*

'Isn't she just perfect?' Percy said as soon as he and Lenny were alone.

'Apart from the not being able to cook thing.' Lenny laughed. 'That could prove a bit of a problem if you really are serious about her.'

'Oh, I'm serious all right.' Percy lit a cigarette and shook out the match. 'In fact, I've never been more serious in my life.'

'In that case, you're going to have to find work somehow. I know you're trying, but a woman like that isn't going to want to shack up in our back bedroom.'

'Don't you think I know that?' The soppy smile left Percy's face. 'There's hardly anything about, though, and whenever I hear of a job, I find a queue of men a mile long competing for it. Winnie even tried to get me an orderly's job at the hospital, but they aren't taking any on. The way it's going, I might have to throw my hand in with Fisk and his gang and start robbing shops.'

Lenny laughed along with Percy and hoped it really was a joke. The pilfering from the docks was bad enough but getting involved with that crowd could only end one way, and Winnie didn't strike him as the sort to wait around if Percy ended up behind bars.

27 - Wednesday 9 June 1926

It was one of those days when it was hard to decide between a sun hat and an umbrella, not that Laura actually had an umbrella. In the sky, a battle was raging between patches of clear blue and billowing black. Unfortunately, the black appeared to be winning. A line of particularly nasty looking cloud was moving slowly across the horizon like a fleet of battleships on a grey, stormy sea. With any luck, she'd get her shopping over and done with before the heavens opened again, although there was no real guarantee. The roads were awash from the last heavy shower and, in places, muddy enough to be slippery. She looked down at her feet and picked her way along carefully, having already had two heart-stopping slips. The butcher's shop was her last port of call. As she went towards the door, her eyes were so fixed on the progress of the battleship clouds that she almost walked into Hetty Porter coming out.

'Oh, good, I was hoping to bump into you.' Hetty smiled and shifted her basket from one arm to the other. Laura couldn't help admiring her grey woollen coat. It was double-breasted and had a wide fur collar and cuffs. She also couldn't help noticing that a few drops of rain had started to fall.

'Do you have another order for me?' She hoped so, because she'd had no new orders since finishing Mrs Wilson's christening shawl, and with Percy not working, they really needed the money.

'I think Rose might be after some more school pinafores for Violet, but it was actually Percy I wanted to see you about. Is he still looking for work?'

'Does the pope wear a funny hat?' Laura sighed. 'There are so many men out of work it's an impossible task, especially for Percy. If he's not queuing for jobs, he's standing in line for his dole money. If he passed a queue outside a shop, he'd probably join it out of habit.'

'I thought as much.' Hetty nodded knowingly. 'The thing is, Bert's cousin, Frank, has been saying he's getting too old for running the little boats in and out of the docks at night. He's decided to branch out and has bought a motorised lorry. The trouble is, Bert doesn't like driving for too long what with his foot. You know he lost all his toes in the war?'

'Mmmm.' Laura nodded and glanced at the dark clouds. They were getting blacker by the second, and her coat was beginning to soak up the drizzly rain. How buying a lorry would help with getting black market goods out of the docks, and what any of this had to do with Percy was a mystery. She wished Hetty would spit it out, whatever it was, so she could go inside the butchers before the heavens really opened. Hetty never used one word when fifty would do. She'd probably get along well with Percy's Winnie. They were both nice, but they could talk your ears off.

'He suffers something terrible in the winter. Would you believe he says his toes itch, even though he left them in France?

Have you ever heard of such a thing? Anyway, Frank has decided to set up a furniture remover's business, all bona fide you understand. Initially, he asked Bert to go into partnership with him, but, what with his foot, he thinks it would be too much for him humping furniture about. He'd rather keep messing about with the boats down at the wharf. Obviously, moving furniture requires two men, preferably strong ones. Well, I said to Bert, "what about Percy Barfoot? He's used to moving stuff around the docks and packing cargo in ship's holds." Bert put it to Frank, and he thought it was a good idea, if Percy would be interested, of course?'

'I think Percy would bite his hand off.'

'I don't think that will be necessary.' Hetty laughed. 'Just ask him to go round to the wharf on William Street as soon as he can and have a word with Frank.'

As Hetty walked away, the rain stopped. A beam of weak sunshine broke through the cloud to briefly light up the wet street, and, arched over the gasworks, a rainbow shimmered. Perhaps it was going to be a nice day after all. Laura walked through the door of the butcher's shop with a huge smile on her face. Maybe things were finally looking up.

28 - Saturday 19 June 1926

The Bell and Crown was crowded, as it always was on a Saturday night. Percy put his hand in his pocket just to reassure himself there really was money in there and he wasn't dreaming. It felt good to have coins jangling for once, even if there weren't as many as he'd have liked. It was even better not to have to hide behind a pillar nursing one drink, half afraid Amy would spot him and throw him out. He looked across the table at Lenny with his pint and Laura with her glass of stout and the cigarette she'd sneaked out of his packet. She was talking about the miners, but he was basking in the pleasure of being able to buy them drinks for once and was only half listening.

'It seems like everyone has forgotten the miners are still locked out.' Laura closed her eyes and exhaled a plume of smoke with obvious pleasure. 'It's the children I feel sorry for. They say the poor mites are starving. I can't help thinking about Bobby and Gladys. What if I couldn't feed them?'

'Bobby and Gladys are as happy as mudlarks, Lor,' Percy said. 'They're not going to starve. Len and me would never let that happen. As for the miners' children, I put half a crown in the relief fund tin when I bought the drinks.'

'You've got a good heart, Percy, but half a crown won't go far, will it?'

'No, but it was the best I could do. It's very nice to have a job, but so far there doesn't seem to be much money in the furniture removal business.'

If Frank hadn't paid him cash in hand so he could still claim his dole money, he'd have been no better off than he'd been before, but he didn't tell Laura about that because she wouldn't approve. Like Lenny, she preferred everything to be legal and above board. The only time she'd ever come close to doing anything illicit was when they were kids and used to swipe Dad's cigarettes.

'It's early days yet, Percy, give it a chance.' Lenny drained the last drops from his glass and put it on the table.

'Oh, I will. Frank has been more than generous. He gave me a third of the profits, even though he was the one who shelled out for the lorry and put his hand in his pocket to fill it with petrol. It's just that most days we haven't had any jobs to do, and a third of nothing is still nothing. I can manage on it living with you and Lor, but it wouldn't pay the rent or put food on the table for a family.'

'You don't have a family to feed, though.' Laura stubbed out her cigarette with a look of regret.

'But I might one of these days. That's why I'll give this venture a chance and do my best to make it work, but if it doesn't pick up—'

'It's only been a week.' Laura took a sip of her stout. 'These things take time. Besides, it's not as if anyone else is falling over themselves to give you work.'

Percy finished his drink and was about to get up to buy another when Arthur Fisk swaggered over to their table.

'Well, well, well, if it isn't Percy Barfoot as I live and breathe. I haven't seen you in here for so long I thought you'd given up drinking. Seeing as you obviously haven't, why don't you let me buy you a drink, and one for Lenny and his good lady wife, too, of course.'

Arthur had lost none of his arrogance, although Percy couldn't help noticing his checked suit was looking a little the worse for wear. It was baggy at the knee and shiny at the elbow.

'We were just leaving.' Laura shot him one of her best dirty looks, finished the last of her stout in one gulp and picked up her hat. 'It'll be getting dark soon, and we have children to get to bed.'

'Thanks all the same.' Lenny smiled and picked up his own hat.

'Oh, come on, Percy.' Arthur tilted his head to one side with a pleading look. 'Don't you desert me as well. Let me buy you a drink, just to show there are no hard feelings over the strike. Although I still think that if we'd broken a few of them blackleg heads, we might have fared better.'

'Just the one, then.' Percy ignored Laura's angry look and

remained seated. Laura and Lenny pushed their way towards the door while Arthur went off to the bar. Percy stared into his empty glass. He knew Lenny and Laura would have stayed for another drink if Arthur hadn't accosted him. He was annoyed with him, but at the same time curious. If Arthur was so keen to buy him a drink, it must mean he wanted something from him. He never did anything for nothing.

When Arthur came back to the table, he was precariously balancing two beers and two whiskeys. Where did he get the money to flash around like that? Lenny said he'd had no work at the docks, and the chances of finding anything else right now were slim to none.

He put the drinks on the table and slid into the seat beside Percy. 'I hear you've got yourself a cushy little job with Frank Scorey.' He raised his eyebrows suggestively. 'If I know Frank, I doubt it's exactly on the level, eh?'

'Actually, it is.' Percy downed the whiskey in one and grimaced at the taste before picking up the beer. So, that was his game. He thought there were some shady deals he could get in on. Perhaps the money from the stolen cigarettes was beginning to run out. Or maybe he was having trouble selling them.

'So, you're driving round in a big lorry moving furniture now. How's that going?' Arthur tossed back his own whiskey and slammed the glass down on the table.

'Not bad.'

'Much money in it?'

'Not so far, but it's early days yet. How about you? You seem to be doing all right.' Percy nodded at the empty whiskey glasses.

'There are ways and means.' Arthur tapped the side of his nose and took a swig of his beer. 'There's money to be had if you know where to look for it.'

'So, the black market, then, or have you got a proper job?'

'Oh, it's much better than that, more direct – if you get my drift?' Arthur winked, looked around to make sure no one was listening and leaned a little closer to Percy. 'In fact, I might just have a proposition for you to earn a bit of extra cash. A lot of extra cash, actually.'

'I'm all ears.'

29 - Tuesday 22 June 1926

Lenny sipped his hot milk and smiled at Laura. She looked a little pale, but it might just be the light, or maybe she was getting one of her headaches. Despite the warm evening, the hot milk sprinkled with a little sugar and cinnamon was welcome. The children had gone to bed, and he'd have to join them soon, but he was putting it off. That was the trouble with starting work at the crack of dawn; you either went to bed early or you flagged halfway through the shift. Percy was out again, supposedly working. It was an obvious lie. Who wanted furniture moved in the dark? He supposed the customers could be doing a moonlight flit, but if they couldn't afford their rent it was unlikely they had money to pay for removals, or much furniture to move for that matter. Still, it was nice to have time alone with Laura, so he wasn't going to spoil it by mentioning his doubts or what he'd seen earlier.

'When Percy says he's serious about Winnie, how serious do you think he means?' Laura looked up from the sock she was darning. It was dull grey, another one of Bobby's by the look of it. That boy went through clothes as if they grew on trees. 'Are we talking marriage, or just . . . you know?'

'Marriage, definitely; that's why he's so obsessed about money.'

'Oh.' She frowned down at the sock with a look that spoke of disappointment.

'Why? I thought you said you liked her?'

'I do. She's very nice, even if it's hard to get a word in edgewise most of the time. I'm just not sure she's right for Percy. When we were washing up the other Sunday, she was telling me all about her job at the hospital. It was interesting, but she sounded just like Percy used to when he talked about the army. It was all about how she was hoping to be promoted to sister and maybe even matron one day.'

'Perhaps that's what they see in each other. All that ambition attracting? He's the same with this new job, desperate to make it work and make his fortune.'

'Desperate to make enough money to impress Winnie more like. He's never worried about money in his life, unless it was having enough to buy another drink. At least with the army it was all about stripes and medals and pride. And look what happened to him when he had to give it all up. If Winnie actually did marry Percy—'

'They might settle down, have a couple of little ones and realise there's more to life than becoming a matron or a sergeant or earning loads of money. Marriage is the best institution in the world.' He winked at her.

'Leonard McAllen, you say the nicest things.'

It was a relief to see her smile. If Laura was smiling, then all was right with the world.

Laura bit the thread on Bobby's sock, turned it in the right way and picked up its partner. There was silence for a while as she set to work darning again and Lenny sipped his drink. They both worried too much about Percy. In some ways, it was understandable. Laura was closer to him than her other brother and her sisters, and Lenny would be forever grateful to him for the way he'd taken him under his wing in France.

Although the fighting on the Somme was more or less over by the time he got there, it was a frightening, horrific introduction to war for a wide-eyed, innocent eighteen-year-old. Sleeping out in the cold in dugouts with shells bursting, constantly having people shout at him, 'Keep your bloody head down, lad, if you want to keep it on your shoulders', the lice, the rats and the smell left him in a constant state of panic. The other men were much older and more experienced. They did their best to look after him, but Percy, his senior by a mere year, led him gently through the horror and the fear like a big brother. If it weren't for Percy, he might have lost his mind in those first few months. But if Percy did marry Winnie, maybe he could finally relax and let someone else do the worrying.

'You don't think Percy is off somewhere with Arthur Fisk, do you?' Laura looked at the clock on the mantel. It was coming up to ten. 'Only, he was acting peculiar after he came back from the pub last Saturday. I asked him what Fisk wanted, and he said he was just trying to mend bridges after the strike, but I don't believe him. What if he's getting caught up in Fisk's thieving?'

'You know how angry he was when he thought Arthur was involved in the break-ins. I'm sure he wouldn't be part of anything like that.'

Despite what he said, Lenny was beginning to think that was exactly what he was doing. Earlier, on his way back from work, he'd seen Percy going into the pub opposite the train station with Arthur and Jimmy. They hadn't seen him, and he hadn't mentioned it to Laura, but there was something furtive and suspicious about them, as if they were up to no good. The London Hotel was an upmarket establishment, all olive-green tiles and gold lettering. It wasn't the kind of place any of them would normally visit. Was Percy so intent on getting enough money together to woo Winnie that he was letting it cloud his judgement?

Laura's head was bent over her darning. She wove the needle in and out of the ruined sock slowly and carefully, as if she was considering what he'd said. The clock ticked. The wool made a quiet swish as she pulled it through her work. He really should go to bed soon.

'He didn't mind being part of their thieving at the docks, though.' She bit her lip and looked up again.

'That was different. It wasn't about people's livelihoods. He's probably just in some pub chatting with Frank. He's full of tales about the old days and the smugglers in the ferry village. Percy says his family were Romany. Apparently, his mother was the first one to be born in a house.'

'You're probably right.' She gave him a weak smile. 'That whole family like a good gossip. If they all got together, they'd be talking for days. I swear Hetty must breathe through her arse – she'd never have time to draw breath otherwise. Maybe the removal business is beginning to take off. Frank put postcards in lots of shop windows. He even put an advertisement in the *Echo*. You never know, they might make their fortunes out of it.'

'Imagine if they did. Percy might find a place of his own, and we'd have the house to ourselves.'

'If he really does make a fortune, I should hope he'd buy us a nice house of our own. Goodness knows, we deserve it for putting up with him so long.'

30 - Tuesday 22 June 1926

Although they were hidden away in a dim alcove at the back of the lounge of the London Hotel, Percy felt vulnerable. The wood-clad bar was a kind of island sticking out into the centre of the pub, which made it an ideal place for those who didn't want to be seen coming and going. Arthur said it was the most anonymous place to meet because no one they knew drank in there. To Percy's mind, they stuck out like sore thumbs in their shabby docker's clothes and flat caps. He'd rather have gone across the road to The Grapes, where you'd be hard pushed to find a single trilby or bowler hat. This place, with its ornate, green-tiled exterior and fancy gold sign, made him uncomfortable, at least until they got to their dark corner out of view.

'What I don't really get is why bicycles?' Percy sat with his elbow on the table and shaded the scarred side of his face with his hand. He was sure the fancy hat brigade was watching them – he could feel their eyes on him. 'I mean, they're hardly easy to hide.'

'Don't you worry about that,' Arthur said with a supercilious smile. 'We've got that covered. All you need to do is drive.'

'But surely there have to be smaller things?' Percy shook his head. It all sounded too impractical. He wasn't sure they'd really thought it through.

'Oh, there are, but they're just too hard to get at, or too much trouble to sell. Take these for instance.' Arthur got a packet of cigarettes out of his pocket and offered them round. Percy took one. Jimmy shook his head and took a gulp of his pint. 'They're easy to hide and quick to sell, but there's not a lot of profit in them, and it's a lot of work touting them round. We tried the jewellers, but they're too well guarded and the banks lock all their money up in safes. We're not safe crackers. The pubs have got plenty of cash, if you pick the right day, but these days, who knows what's the right day. No bugger's got any money. It's not worth taking the risk for five or ten measly quid. There are eight cycle shops within a two-mile radius of this pub, and each one is stuffed with top-of-the-range machines. They're easy pickings and big profits. We can make maybe five or ten quid on each one, easy.'

'If you can sell them.' Percy raised an eyebrow.

'Oh, we can sell them all right,' Jimmy sneered. 'There's hundreds of dockers and the like who'd be more than happy to buy them off us no questions asked. Imagine being able to get to the dock gate in half the time every morning.'

'But do dockers and the like have that kind of money? That's two or three weeks wages on double shifts.' Percy still wasn't convinced.

'Instalment plans.' Arthur smiled, leaned back in his seat and took a pull on his cigarette. 'They pay us ten shillings or a quid every week. We have regular money coming in. Job done.'

'And if they can't pay?'

'They'll pay.' Jimmy winked, reached inside his jacket and pulled out a cosh, much like the one Arthur had had on the picket line.

'Not in here.' Arthur gave him a hard stare and Jimmy quickly put the weapon away. Then Arthur crossed his legs and leaned forward, as if he was about to inspect the bottom of his shoe. 'You don't need to worry about all the details, Percy. We've already taken care of them. We've been doing this for a long time now. We're not amateurs. I've cased the shop. I know how to get in. I know when to get in. All you have to do is be there with your lorry at the right time and drive to where we tell you. We split the profits four ways, no quibbling.'

'Four ways?' Percy looked pointedly at Arthur and Jimmy.

'Sam's the lookout, but he already knows what he's got to do so there's no point him being here tonight,' Arthur said. 'Now, are you in or not? Because if you're not, you're wasting our fucking time.'

'I'm in.' He needed no time to think.

Percy was glad to get out of the pub. He swore he could feel eyes boring into his back as they sidled outside. Arthur headed up Oxford Street towards The Grapes, Jimmy turned towards Canute Road and the dock gate and he headed down Terminus Terrace towards the bridge. It was best not to be seen together any more than they could help. It had still been light when they entered the pub, but it was dark now. It made him feel safer somehow, but he was still uneasy. A few doors down the road, he stopped outside a boarding house, got his cigarettes out of his pocket and lit one. Nonchalantly, he looked back towards the pub. There was a man in a dark suit and a fedora hat leaning on the tiled wall at the corner of the pub. Was he watching him? He saw the flare of a match as the man lit a cigarette and relaxed a little. All this subterfuge was making him jumpy. He didn't like it, any more than he liked throwing his hand in with Arthur and Jimmy, but it was a necessary evil.

31 - Wednesday 23 June 1926

When Percy kissed Winnie goodnight outside her house, he'd felt as if he was saying goodbye before going off to war. He wanted to cling to her, press her firm little body close, feel her heart beating in time with his and never let her go. Now, sitting in the dark behind the shops on West Marlands Road reminded him of waiting to go over the top. There was no mud, no smell of death, no whizz-bangs shaking the ground as they exploded, and he had no rifle, helmet, gas mask or pack, but the feeling of anticipation was the same. In a funny way, it made him feel alive, just as it had back then in France. His senses tingled and, despite the darkness, everything was bright and clear in his mind. The fact that the lorry had seen use with the Service Corps in France added to his feeling of being back in the war. From the cab, he looked across at the park. According to Winnie, there'd been a leper hospital here once. Now it was just a shabby park of balding grass surrounded by a line of trees that at least had the advantage of hiding him from view.

It had been a fairly warm day, but the temperature had dropped when the sun set, and he felt the chill. He pulled the collar of his jacket towards his ears and blew on his hands. There was nothing to do but wait, just like in the trenches, but at least there he'd had some company. Now he was alone, slumped in the cab with his cap pulled down over his eyes. To a passing observer, it would look as if he was parked up having a nap. Not that there was likely to be anyone passing now. Arthur said he'd been monitoring the area for weeks and knew exactly when the local bobby came past on his beat. Two thirty was, he said, the optimum time; Wednesday was the optimum day because of half day closing. To give him credit, he'd certainly done his homework.

Frank had fitted wing mirrors to the truck to make it easier to drive. Percy looked in the one to his right and saw Sam Strange leaning against the wall behind the back doors of the cycle shop, smoking a cigarette and trying to look nonchalant. He seemed nervous, with his tapping foot and his head turning this way and that. It struck Percy as odd that they should choose a watchman with such an obvious defect. Still, even if his eyes didn't work properly, those great big ears must be good for listening out. He had an idea Sam had only been included because of his friendship with Jimmy. They'd been in the workhouse together as boys. Poor old Sam had been left on the church doorstep as a foundling, or so he said, and Jimmy had ended up there when he was ten, after his father beat his mother to death. Maybe Sam had taken care of Jimmy when he first arrived, much like he'd done with Lenny in France.

He stole a glance at his watch. It was almost a quarter to three. What was taking them so long? He'd have expected them to come out with the first bicycles by now, but there'd been no movement at all. Maybe something had gone wrong. It seemed unlikely after all of Arthur's careful planning, but the last thing he wanted was for the shop owner, Mr Apsey, to end up like poor old

Mr Petheridge from the newsagents. He didn't want to be involved in that kind of thing, even from a safe distance. Then, right when he'd begun to think they'd set him up in some way and left him out in the lorry like a sitting duck, he heard the creak of a door opening. He glanced into the mirror again, and sure enough, there was Jimmy pushing a bicycle out into the street. It was action time.

32 - Wednesday 23 June 1926

The chill in the bedroom kept Laura awake. Beside her, Lenny snored away, sleeping like a baby. She envied him. He could probably sleep standing up at a bus stop. Lately, she struggled, no matter how tired she was. She'd put an extra blanket on the bed, but her feet were still cold, and no matter which way she turned, the mattress felt lumpy and uncomfortable. During the day, she wandered around like an automaton, barely able to think properly or keep her eyes open, but as soon as she went to bed, she was wide-awake. Her mind just wouldn't seem to switch off.

No matter how much she tried to deny it to herself, she knew she was paying the price for those heady mornings during the strike, when she and Lenny had been all alone in the house. They'd been careful. They were always careful. Not careful enough, though, obviously. For weeks now, she'd been telling herself it wasn't happening, blaming the stress of the strike, not eating properly, worrying about Percy, and anything else she could think of. Now, it was undeniable. Soon, there was going to be another mouth to feed.

Between feeling sick and needing to use the jerry under the bed, she worried. Mostly, she worried about how they were going to cope with another baby. For a start, there was no room in the house. They might just be able to squeeze a crib into the corner of the bedroom, but there were four of them sleeping in it already, and a baby waking up and crying several times in the night wouldn't be good for any of them. If it hadn't been for the strike, they might have been able to save enough money to move somewhere bigger and better, but they'd lost around two weeks' wages, plus the money they'd missed out on while Percy was looking for work, and there was no way of catching up on that quickly. Of course, if it hadn't been for the strike, they might not be in this position at all.

A new baby took up so much time and energy. It might not cost anything to feed it, at least at first, but there was all the extra time she'd have to spend washing nappies and baby clothes. When would she ever find the time to sew or knit and make the extra pennies to squirrel away in the emergency tin? How on earth had her mother coped with six children? She hadn't told her yet, although, last week, she'd kept giving her funny looks, so she may already have an idea. If anyone was qualified to spot the signs of pregnancy, it was her mother. Lenny and Percy were still blissfully unaware, but that was more understandable. If she didn't tell them, the chances of either of them noticing anything before she gave birth were pretty slim. Percy might start telling her she was getting fat, but that was about as much as he'd grasp. Lenny wouldn't even see that, or, if he did, he'd never say anything.

She hadn't heard Percy come in yet, and that was another worry. He and Frank were getting a bit more work now, they'd even got a couple of regular jobs transporting things for furniture shops, but Percy had been on edge of late. She was concerned he was going to walk away from the business because he wasn't yet earning enough money. If he did, he'd never find another job. She'd become used to him being out all hours when he started walking Winnie home from work, and, wherever else he'd been going in the evenings, he hadn't been coming home drunk, so she had no right to complain. Even so, she couldn't help thinking there was something dodgy going on. It must be after three o'clock now, and he still wasn't home. Where the hell was he?

33 - Thursday 24 June 1926

Percy watched through the mirror of the truck as Jimmy handed the first bicycle to Sam and then went back through the back door of the shop. A few moments later, he reappeared with another one. Arthur was right behind him with yet another. The trio wheeled them towards the back of the lorry. Percy smiled. It was all going to plan; maybe a little later than he'd expected, but to plan all the same. He sat perfectly still; his head turned slightly to the right so he could see what they were doing in the mirror. He could feel his heart racing. Arthur's plan was for the three of them to load as many bicycles into the lorry as they could, then Jimmy and Arthur would get into the cab. He didn't know where they were meant to go from there. Presumably, Arthur had somewhere organised to store the bicycles, but he hadn't shared that information with him so far. Maybe he didn't quite trust him yet.

As soon as Percy lost sight of Arthur, Jimmy and Sam, he banged his foot three times on the floor of the cab. Moments later, all hell broke loose, and Percy's smile grew wider.

34 - Thursday 24 June 1926

Lenny stood at the kitchen door with a sick feeling in the pit of his stomach. Laura was at the table with her head in her hands. Her breath came in ragged gasps. She was crying. She wasn't the kind of woman who cried at the drop of a hat, so something was obviously badly wrong, although he had no idea what. She must have sensed him there because she looked up. Her eyes were red and puffy, her beautiful hair was sticking up everywhere and she looked terrible.

'What's wrong? What's happened?' He crossed the room, knelt and enfolded her in his arms.

'It's Percy.' She wiped at her eyes with the back of her hand and buried her face in his chest. 'He didn't come home at all last night. I'm sure something terrible has happened to him.'

'Are you sure he didn't just go out early? Maybe they had a job—' It sounded lame even as he started to say it.

'I'm sure.' She got up stiffly and put the kettle on the range. 'I couldn't sleep last night because you were snoring. If he'd come in, I'd have heard him. I've even checked his room. Ever since he stayed in the pub with Arthur Fisk, I've known something was wrong. He's got himself involved in something dodgy with that lot, and now he's probably got arrested. If it's burgling shops, Frank won't like it. He'll likely lose his job.'

Lenny sat at the table and rubbed his knuckles across his mouth. He wanted to tell her she was wrong, that Percy wouldn't do something like that, but he wasn't sure it was true. He couldn't forget seeing him going through the door of the London Hotel with Arthur Fisk and Jimmy Pothecary. He'd known they were up to something, and, as much as he didn't want to believe it, everything pointed in one direction.

'Maybe we should wait until he gets home and ask him? Anything could have happened.'

'Like what? Are we supposed to hope he might have been run down by a tram, or beaten up and robbed, or—'

At that moment, Percy waltzed through the door as if nothing had happened. He smiled at them, but he looked worse than Laura. His clothes were crumpled, his eyes were heavy and he badly needed a shave. He removed his cap and stepped into the room.

'Where the bloody hell have you been?' Laura jumped up, slapped his face and began to cry again.

Percy put his arms around her. 'I've been at the police station.'

'I knew it!' Laura pulled away from him. 'You've got yourself involved with Arthur bloody Fisk and now you've been arrested. You stupid, stupid idiot.' She began to pound on his chest, but he caught her hands.

'Thanks for the vote of confidence, Lor.'

He sank into the nearest chair, leaned his head back and closed his eyes. The kettle began to whistle. Lenny went to the range and began to make the tea, although what he wanted was an explanation, not a drink. He didn't know what to think or what to say.

No one said anything. Percy sat completely still with his eyes closed. Laura sat beside him and stared miserably into space. Lenny put cups in front of them and went back to the range to fetch his own. When he sat down, Percy opened his eyes.

'I wasn't at the police station because I'd been arrested.' He took a long gulp from the teacup. The tea was still so hot it must have burned his mouth, but he showed no sign of it. 'I was there making a statement.'

'About what?' Laura looked as if she was in pain. Lenny reached across the table and took her hand. He hated to see her like this.

'Arthur bloody Fisk, amongst other things.' Percy raised one eyebrow and gave Laura a sarcastic smile.

Lenny should have been having breakfast and getting ready for work before the children got up, but work was the last thing on his mind. Instead, he sat with his elbows on the table, watched his tea get cold and listened as Percy's tale unfolded. He explained how, at the end of May, he'd overheard Arthur talking to Jimmy and Sam in the pub and decided to follow them. He said he knew they were involved in the break-in at Jones's tobacconist, but he also knew he needed proof before he could go to the police.

'You should have told me. I could have helped.' Lenny's conscience pricked for thinking the worst. Percy shouldn't have had to tackle them alone. They were family. He should have felt able to ask for help.

'I didn't want you involved in it, Len. Anyway, it came to nothing because that was the night I bumped into Winnie, and after that I got a bit distracted.' He smiled sheepishly. 'Then Arthur came to me the other night in the pub. He told me about a robbery he was planning. It was a bicycle shop. He needed a driver, and he asked me to help.'

'And you still didn't think to tell me, or Laura?'

'The first person I told was Charlie West. I went to him the next day and told him exactly what I thought that lot had been up to, and what they were planning to get up to. He believed me, but he said there was nothing he could do without evidence. So, between us, we cooked up a plan to get it. I let Arthur think I was going along with him and, just like Charlie instructed, I told no one about it. Well, no one except Frank. I had to tell him because I didn't want to take the lorry without his permission. If I'd told you and it had all gone wrong, then you and Laura and the kids would have been involved in it, too.'

Percy drained the rest of his tea and wiped his mouth with the back of his hand.

'So, the robbery was last night, then?' Laura turned to him with a watery smile.

'Yes, at half past two, or three o'clock by the time it all actually happened. It was in Above Bar. I waited in the van at the back of the shop behind West Marlands Park. It was all exactly as Arthur had planned, except for the five constables hiding in the back of the lorry. As soon as I spotted Arthur, Jimmy and Sam coming out with the bicycles, I gave the signal to alert them, and that was that. There was a bit of a scuffle by the sound of it, but all three of them were arrested.'

'Crooks don't like grasses, Percy. They're going to be after your blood.' Lenny couldn't help wondering if it was all worth it. They wouldn't be in prison forever and, when they got out, he'd be looking over his shoulder for the rest of his life.

'They already are. You should have heard them screaming at me as they were carted off. They don't scare me, though.'

That was half Percy's trouble. Nothing scared him. He thought he was invincible, but Lenny was worried all the same.

'So, if all this happened at three o'clock, why has it taken you so long to come home?' Lenny asked.

Surely it didn't take that long to give a statement and get back from the police station. It was next to the Bargate, no more than a mile away.

'Well, it took a while to give my statement. Then, when Charlie took Fisk's fingerprints and told me what he'd found—'

'What do you mean, what he'd found?' Laura's look was a mixture of confusion and horror.

'After I heard about Mr Petheridge being beaten half to death that night on Onslow Road, I got to thinking. I mean, it was a robbery gone wrong; the robbers hit the shop owner over the head and emptied the cash box. It all sounded a lot like what happened to Maria's Fred. That was why I was so keen to catch the buggers. Part of me thought I was adding two and two and making six, but I told Charlie what I thought all the same. He only half believed it himself. The three of them are crooks, no doubt about it, and they all like a ruck, but it's a big step from that to murder. Anyway, all three of them were fingerprinted at the station, and Charlie went straight off to check them against the prints from Fred's case. He didn't expect to find anything, any more than I did really, but I waited just in case. I could hardly believe it when he came back and told me that Fisk's prints matched. He killed Fred.'

35 - Thursday 24 June 1926

Mum's face when she saw the three of them standing on her
doorstep was a combination of horror, anger and bewilderment.
Laura couldn't blame her. She'd felt much the same when Charlie
West knocked on her door earlier. She'd been dozing in the parlour,
Lenny had gone to work and Percy was in bed catching up on lost
sleep. She vaguely remembered Charlie from school, but she couldn't
fathom why he was there. Surely, he didn't need more information
from Percy already. Then he explained he was going to break the
news about Arthur Fisk to Maria. He thought Percy might want to go
along, too.

'Oh, Percy,' Mum cried. 'What have you done now?'

Poor Percy looked at his feet, his face a picture of misery. He
still hadn't shaved, so the bottom half looked as if it had been down a
coal mine. The top was pale from lack of sleep, and his scar was a
vivid slash between the two. How must it feel to have your own
mother always think the worst of you? Laura decided she was no
better, either. Hadn't she accused him of being a thief just this
morning? He must feel the whole world was against him, even when
he did the right thing.

'This is my friend, Constable Charlie West.' Percy's voice was
quiet and hoarse. 'He has some news for Maria.'

With a grim face, Mum shoved them all along the hallway and through the back parlour door. Maria looked up from her knitting; socks this time, by the look of it. Her eyes narrowed and darted between Percy and Charlie. At least she didn't accuse Percy of anything, well, not out loud. While Percy made the introductions, Mum pushed Laura into the empty armchair opposite Maria before slumping in the remaining one. Percy and Charlie stood awkwardly. Charlie took off his helmet and ran his hand nervously through what was left of his sandy hair. It had receded badly at the temples, as if his shiny forehead was making a break for freedom and trying to re-join the equally shiny island at his crown. After clearing his throat a few times, Charlie began his tale. He explained the ambush of the previous night, including Percy's part in it. Mum's expression slowly went from shame at doubting her son to pride for what he'd done. Maria looked more confused than ever, with her knitting in her lap and her wet, brown eyes wide. She obviously couldn't work out what this all had to do with her.

'The thing is.' Charlie twisted his helmet in his hands anxiously. 'Not only did Percy here help us to stop their three-man crimewave, but he also had an idea about an older crime they might have been involved in. The robbery in the newsagents reminded him of the bakery robbery last year—'

Maria let out a sound that was somewhere between a squeal and a whimper. She put her hand over her mouth.

Charlie, looking more uncomfortable than ever, continued.

'Because of Percy's suspicions, I checked the fingerprints of all three men against the ones from the cash box in Fred's case. Arthur Fisk's were a match. He'll be appearing in court today to be officially charged with Fred's murder.'

'So, he'll hang?' Maria's voice was a squeak, and her eyes were brimming over with tears.

'If we can make a good case before the assizes in July.' Charlie's ruddy face got redder. 'He's denied everything except the attempted robbery last night, and he can hardly deny that when he was caught in the act. He says he was courting a girl who worked at the bakery, and they met there after hours once or twice. That's when he says his fingerprints must have got there. We have to speak to the girl, of course, but the fact the prints were inside the cash box doesn't look good for him.'

'But he could still get away with it?' Mum frowned.

'Unless he confesses, it's a remote possibility.' Charlie looked at Percy uneasily. 'The fingerprints are very damning, though. They prove he was there, and it will be hard for him to convince a jury why they would be inside the cash box if he didn't empty it. Twenty years ago, the Stratton brothers hanged because of very similar evidence. It would be helpful if Mr Petheridge was able to identify him, but, so far, he can't remember anything except that the robbers had scarves over their faces.'

Laura had a horrible sinking feeling. The way Charlie looked at Percy, and all his ifs and buts, made her nervous. She was certain Fisk really had killed Fred, but would a jury see it that way? They didn't know what a nasty piece of work he was, and it sounded as if he had all his excuses lined up ready. What if the girl he was courting was in on it, too? Percy had put his own neck on the line to bring the three of them to book. If it all turned out to be a waste of time and Fisk got off, he'd be gunning for Percy. How much danger would he be in?

36 - Tuesday 29 June 1926

The crowd of men leaving the dock gate scattered in different directions like rats with a cat in their nest. By the time Lenny reached the edge of the park, they'd thinned out considerably and he was no longer carried along by the tide of bodies. Some headed up towards God's House, some down Canute Road, others crossed the park. Lenny watched them peel off as he made his way towards the corner of Terminus Terrace. The grass that had been so green back in May was bare and muddy in places, churned up by dockers' boots. It had been a wet, cold summer so far. When he reached the corner of Oxford Street, he heard someone call his name and turned to see Charlie West standing outside the station like the laughing policemen in the music hall song. With a smile, Lenny crossed the road and left the last of the dockers behind.

'Hello, Charlie, still on the beat? After you solved our recent crimewave, I'd have thought they'd have promoted you.' He liked Charlie and, keen as he was to get home, didn't mind stopping to pass the time of day.

'No such luck,' Charlie grinned. 'Maybe once the trial's over. How's Percy?'

'He's fine.' Out of all of them, Percy was the only one who seemed unfazed by the weight of the trial hanging over them. Since the story of the arrest had appeared in the *Echo*, everyone was talking about what he'd done. Most were hailing him as something of a local hero, although he'd overheard an undercurrent of resentment from certain quarters about betraying three of their own. Percy didn't seem to care about any of it, though.

'Business is picking up, or so he says. I think he and Frank might really be able to make a go of this venture.'

'That's good to hear. And he hasn't had any trouble?' Charlie's face gave nothing away, but there was obviously something behind the question.

'What do you mean by trouble?' He felt a tightening in his stomach and a prickle of alarm. Had someone made a threat? Was Percy in danger?

'Nothing really.' Charlie rubbed nervously at his chin. 'It's just that we had a visit from Mrs Fisk. For a woman who has spent the last eight years telling her son he wasn't fit to wipe his dead brother's boots, she's certainly changed her tune. By the way she's going on now, you'd think her little Arthur was an angel terribly wronged by the world. According to her, it's everyone's fault but Arthur's. She started off saying Sam and Jimmy led him astray. She called them "those workhouse boys." Then she said Percy was the mastermind and had set poor Arthur up.' Charlie looked at his feet.

'She said that?' Now he really was concerned. It was one thing to mutter about Percy being a grass but accusing him of being behind the burglaries was something else altogether.

'Don't worry, no one's taking any notice of her.' Charlie held his hand up as if he was stopping traffic. 'It's only the ranting of a broken-hearted mother. I just wanted to be sure she hadn't been giving Percy any grief.'

'Not that I know of.' Would Percy have told him if she had? He'd kept him in the dark about everything else. 'Do you think I should warn him?'

'I doubt she'll go anywhere near him. I told her spouting nonsense like that would make it even worse for Arthur. Not that it could really be any worse for him. It was all probably just hot air. If Percy does have any trouble from her, though, let me know and I'll have another word.'

'I suppose Arthur is sticking to his story, then?'

'Like shit to an army blanket. We have them all bang to rights for the bicycle shop break-in, though. Arthur and Jimmy have admitted it, but young Sam says he was just walking past and stopped to help out. He says he didn't realise it was a robbery. If that boy had a brain, he'd be dangerous.'

'What about the other thing?' He wasn't worried about the burglary, or Jimmy and Sam. Arthur and what he'd done to poor old Fred was his only concern.

'The arrogant little idiot really thinks he'll get away with it if he just keeps saying he didn't do it, and he's never burgled anywhere before, either. That's where Percy's statement comes in. Arthur boasted to him about breaking into tobacconists, pubs and jeweller's shops. In the end, his big mouth is what's going to put the noose around his neck. The girl Arthur was courting has been questioned, too. She's confirmed they did meet in the bakery after hours once or twice, but she can't remember Arthur ever being anywhere near the cash box. He dropped her right after the robbery, too, and that doesn't look good. In the end, it will be down to what the jury believes, but the fact he was caught red handed this time, and that he and Jimmy both had coshes on them, looks bad for him. We found a whole load of cigarettes in both Arthur and Jimmy's rooms, too. They say they bought them from a man in a pub, but it's hardly believable. There was nothing incriminating at Sam's house, apart from his mother.'

'His mother? I thought he was a foundling?'

'He was, but this woman says she's his mother. She's fed him some line about him being stolen from his pram and he's believed it, as if someone would steal a baby and then leave it on the steps of the church. She's a right piece of work, I can tell you. It looks like she saw him as an easy target and has been living off him for months. Anyway, there was nothing at all in his house. Barely anything to say he had ever lived there. She'd seen the writing on the wall and had either sold or pawned most of what he owned by the time we got there.'

'Poor Sam.' Out of all of them, Sam was the only one Lenny

felt sorry for. Arthur and Jimmy had both used him, and now it sounded as if this woman had, too. The poor lad didn't have the brains he was born with. 'Have they said anything else?'

'Jimmy's trying to say it was all Arthur's idea, and young Sam really thinks a jury's going to believe he was just passing by at three o'clock in the morning and being helpful. He's the weakest link. They'll tie him up in knots in the dock.'

Lenny left Charlie and carried on towards home with an uneasy feeling about what he'd learned. He climbed the steps of the railway bridge without really noticing where he was going. Charlie said Mrs Fisk was just ranting, trying to save her son. In a way, it was understandable. She'd lost three sons in the war and now it looked as if she was going to lose her last one to the noose. She was probably desperate and grasping at straws. The whole story was ridiculous. Why would Percy mastermind a robbery and then tell the police? The trouble was, with Percy's reputation for drinking and fighting, his legendary temper and the way he looked, people might give it some credence. These kinds of rumours had a way of getting out of hand. What if people actually began to believe her?

37 - Wednesday 7 July 1926

It was odd to think that for the other people in this strange little pub, this was just another day. The toothless old man in the moth-eaten cap on the bench by the window looked as if he sat in the exact same place every morning with his newspaper. The barman, with his handlebar moustache and pocket watch, probably always served him and didn't think the ancient building, which was all low ceilings, dark beams and crooked walls, was anything special. Even in the court, most of the people they'd seen had been simply going about their usual business. Justice Roche, the ushers and the clerks were merely doing their normal jobs, and the imposing, church-like stone and flint building was nothing more to them than a place of work. The gawpers in the public gallery were likely locals who visited each of the Winchester assizes for their entertainment. To them, it was the same as going to a play or the picture house.

Laura looked across the table at Maria. At least she'd stopped crying now. As much as Laura felt out of her depth in this strange city of narrow passages and unfamiliar shops, it was nothing to how Maria must feel. At the start, the pomp and circumstance of the proceedings had taken their minds off why they were there. Justice Roche had a kindly face, and his strange wig and gown were almost comical. Laura had to resist the urge to giggle. They'd watched with interest as the clerk selected the jurors and read out the names of the defendants and witnesses. Then Percy's name was called out and it all began to seem personal. When Arthur Fisk, Jimmy Pothecary and Sam Strange were brought to the dock and the charges were read out, the dark-haired woman in black on the opposite side of the gallery began to mop at her wide blue eyes. There was something familiar about her.

'Isn't that Fisk's mother?' Maria whispered. Then she began to weep herself. Whether it was through pity for Mrs Fisk, the arrogant looks on Fisk and Pothecary's faces or hearing Fred's name, Laura couldn't tell. That was when they'd left the court.

'I knew I shouldn't have come.' Maria sipped at the glass of medicinal brandy Frank had bought her. She was dressed all in black, from her boots to her turban-style hat. It made her face look paler and her eyes look redder. 'I'm sorry for making such a spectacle of myself.'

'Nonsense.' Frank patted her hand. He was smaller than Laura had expected. Percy made him sound larger than life, but he was no more than five foot four, and lean with it. Although he was wearing his Sunday best and his jet-black hair was a neat short back and sides, his thick brows and leathery, weather-beaten face revealed his gypsy blood. 'I'm sure no one even noticed.'

'If you hadn't come, you'd have regretted it,' Laura said.

'It was his face that set me off. That smug smirk, as if he knew he was going to get away with it. That and his poor mother having to live with the shame. All I could see was him looking down at my dear Fred with that same smirk on his face. When I saw his mother crying, I couldn't bear it for one more second. Maybe I'd have handled it better if I'd had more time to prepare. It's all happened so quickly. How can it be that just two weeks ago I'd never heard of this man, and now he's on trial for murdering my husband? It makes no sense to me.'

'I know.' Two weeks ago, Laura's biggest worry was the hole in her roof and the baby in her belly. How things had changed. 'At least the timing was good. Imagine if they'd planned the robbery two weeks later. We'd have had it hanging over us until the lent assizes, or have had to go to London to the Old Bailey. Today, or tomorrow, it will all be over, and you'll never have to think about Fisk walking around free again.'

'What if he gets away with it, though?' Maria took another sip of brandy.

'He won't.' Laura looked at the glass of stout on the table in front of her, but she didn't pick it up. Her stomach was tied up in knots. If she drank it right now, she'd likely be sick. 'You know the evidence they've got. There's the fingerprints inside the cash box, the coshes they were carrying and Percy's statement about the other robberies.'

'How long do you think it will be?' Maria began to bite at the skin around her fingernails.

'Your guess is as good as mine.' Laura shook her head. 'Percy will come and find us as soon as he can, though. Charlie knows where we are.'

38 - Wednesday 7 July 1926

Percy decided he didn't like Winchester. In Southampton, he never had to think about where he was going or how he was going to get there. He knew every street, every bridge and every shortcut. Here he felt all at sea, which was ironic as he was further from the coast than he'd ever been in his life, if you didn't count France. He quickly found the stone gate he was supposed to walk through. Charlie had said it was a bit like the Bargate, but smaller. He was right about that much. Now he had to keep going downhill until he saw something called the Buttercross. Apparently, it was some kind of tall, spiky monument with steps at the bottom. So far, all he'd seen were shops shut for half-day closing and people staring at him. What was wrong with them? Hadn't they ever seen a man with a scar on his face before?

He'd been pleased when he saw Laura, Maria and Frank get up and leave the court. It looked as if Maria was crying. He hadn't wanted them to hear his statement, or all that stuff about the number of blows to poor Fred's head and the fractures to his skull, especially with Fisk and Pothecary smirking the whole time. It might have been better if Maria hadn't come at all. It was a mercy she'd left before the defence lawyer started making his case, calling all their evidence circumstantial and saying the fingerprints only proved Fisk had been in the bakery, which he'd already admitted. Percy had a job not to laugh when the young woman Arthur had been courting threw a spanner in the works by saying she was sure he'd never been near the cash box.

'Mr Chubb was particular about keeping it in the drawer under the counter,' she'd said. 'He would never have left it out.' The glare Arthur gave her didn't help his case.

The high street seemed to go on forever. It was far narrower than Southampton High Street. The buildings crowded in on him, and there were little side streets and passageways everywhere. He began to think he might have missed the monument somehow. Then, as he was about to turn back and retrace his steps, he saw it, and the passageway behind it, which was like a tunnel between the shops. This place was worse than the rabbit warren of trenches on the Western Front. He'd be glad to get back home. Now, had Charlie said turn left or turn right? He looked around anxiously. 'You can't miss it,' Charlie had said. Ah, there it was, The Eclipse Inn. It was a rather warped looking building, all mullioned windows and bent beams. Winchester seemed to be filled with similar places. If she'd been with him, Winnie would have probably told him its history. He wouldn't have minded being lost if she was on his arm.

The inside of the pub was gloomy. It took a moment for his eyes to adjust after the bright sunshine outside. It was also almost empty. There was just the barman, an old man reading a newspaper and Laura, Maria and Frank huddled around a table.

Frank saw him first. 'Let me get you a drink, Percy, you look as if you could use one.'

'But you've already lost a day's work driving us all here in Bert's motorcar.'

'Nonsense. Without you, I'd never have been able to do any work anyway, and this was far more important.'

He conceded defeat and sat between Laura and Maria. They both looked at him expectantly.

'Is it all over?' Laura asked.

'Yes, and I never want to go through something like that again, even if I live to be a hundred.'

'Was it bad?' Maria put her hand on his arm and looked as if she was going to start crying again.

'Well, it wasn't good. At least most of it wasn't. Their lawyer tried to make them out to be desperate victims of the strike, who had fallen on hard times and were almost starving. It might have worked better if Fisk and Pothecary hadn't looked so smug the whole time. The only one I felt sorry for was Sam. He was so bewildered I began to think the lawyer should have said he was mentally defective. He'd have got off easily if he had.'

Frank came back with the first of the drinks, and while he went back for the others, Percy got his cigarettes out. He offered the packet to Laura. After a moment's hesitation, she took one.

'So, how long do you think the jury will take?' Frank asked as he sat back down.

'They've already come back. If I hadn't stopped to chat to Charlie and get directions here, I'd have missed the verdict.'

He didn't mention the brief encounter with Fisk's mother, her tears, or the slap to his face. He didn't blame her. Whatever Arthur had done, he was still her son. When she'd slapped him, he wondered if his mother would have tried quite so hard to believe his innocence. Somehow, he doubted it.

'So, it's really over?' Laura looked as if she didn't believe him.

'Yes. They were out for less than twenty minutes. They found them guilty on all counts.'

Maria began to weep again, and Laura's face said she didn't know whether to laugh or join her.

'So, Fisk will hang?' Maria dabbed at her eyes.

'Yes. When the judge put the black cloth on his head, it certainly wiped the smile off Fisk's face. I thought he was going to cry. Poor old Sam did cry. He got five years and Pothecary got seven. He was the only one that kept his composure. He just shut his eyes for a moment and carried on smiling. Anyone would have thought he wanted to go to prison.'

39 - Saturday 10 July 1926

Queens Park was swarming with people; all ages and classes were packed together competing for a view of Platform Road. Laura would rather not have come. The last thing she wanted to do was spend the afternoon standing about in the heat watching the bloody Hospital Carnival, but Percy had insisted. He said they all needed some fun after the last few weeks, and the children would enjoy it. In truth, he wanted to go because Winnie was on one of the floats. They'd arrived early to get a good spot. Now, latecomers had squashed them against the railings like sardines. The heat of all the bodies and the combined smell of their sweat and cologne made Laura feel faintly nauseous. She didn't like crowds at the best of times, but in this sticky heat, they were intolerable.

Percy was right about the children; they loved it. Gladys could hardly contain her excitement as the first of the brightly coloured floats came into view. Percy had given them a few pennies to put in the collection buckets, and he lifted them over the railings so they could get a better view.

'I'm going to put my pennies in Winnie's bucket when she comes.' Gladys jumped up and down excitedly. 'They're going to build a new bit of hospital with them.'

'It's called an extension, silly.' Bobby shot her a look that was part smugness, part disgust at her stupidity. 'And it won't be built out of pennies, they're just using them to pay for it.'

'Well, Uncle Percy said they're going to use our pennies to build it.' She crossed her arms sulkily and turned her back on him.

Laura couldn't help laughing; their squabbling reminded her so much of her and Percy at that age. Then the Thorneycroft's band came past playing jazz music and Gladys forgot about being cross and began to dance instead.

Once Winnie's float had gone past and they'd waved and cheered at her in her Harlequin costume, Laura decided she'd done her duty. She felt so sick and headachy she'd probably have gone home right then, but Lenny had said he'd meet them in the park after work. Instead, she told Percy she was getting too hot and left him to watch Bobby and Gladys while she went to find some shade. She shoved her way through the crowd and was relieved to find the far side of the park fairly empty. Better still, there was an unoccupied bench over in the far corner by the Gordon Memorial. If memory served, it was the one she and Lenny had sat on during the strike. She hurried to it and sank down, grateful for the shadow of the trees.

She closed her eyes and tried hard not to think about why she felt so terrible. Soon, she'd have to tell Lenny about the baby, but talking about it would make it more real. He'd likely be happy, but whichever way you looked at it, another mouth to feed was a worry he didn't need. When she opened her eyes again, an olive-skinned man in a dark, pinstriped suit and trilby hat was standing in front of her.

'Excuse me, do you mind if I sit here?'

'Of course not.'

She didn't own the bench and, by the look of him, he could afford to buy it ten times over if he wished. The fabric and stitching of the suit spoke of quality. It must have cost a pretty penny. The man smiled and sat down. He looked to be about her brother Willy's age; late thirties or early forties. He had a long, narrow face with an overhanging brow that cast his small, dark eyes into shadow and long, narrow dimples, which were like brackets on either side of his mouth, even when his smile faded. It was a strong face but not unpleasant.

'I didn't want to be presumptuous. I imagined you were waiting for someone. I should hate to intrude, or worse still, have your sweetheart arrive and think I was making advances.'

'Goodness me.' Laura could feel a blush rising. 'It's been a long time since I had a sweetheart. I'm waiting for my husband to finish work while my children watch the parade.'

'You look too young to have children, especially ones old enough to be off watching the parade on their own.'

He was well spoken and polite, but she had the feeling he might be secretly laughing at her.

'They're with my brother. He's better with crowds than me. I got a bit overheated.'

'I know what you mean.' He nodded, and those dimples deepened. 'It's very humid today. I'm afraid I overestimated my endurance, too. It's nice here in the shade, though, even if we can't see much of the parade. I hear the Sea Cadets have a sailboat on wheels.'

'Actually, I don't really mind missing it. It was my brother who wanted to see it, and the children, too, of course.'

The man reached into his jacket pocket, pulled out a pipe and then looked at her uncertainly. 'Do you mind if I smoke? I know some ladies don't like the smell very much. It does tend to cling to your clothes.'

'I don't mind at all.'

With a lot of puffing and sucking, he lit his pipe then held out his hand and said, 'Sorry, it's remiss of me not to introduce myself. I'm Edgar Fielding.'

'Laura McAllen.' She took his hand and shook it awkwardly.

'It's a wonderful idea to raise money for the hospital like this, isn't it?' He gestured towards the crowd with his pipe.

'Yes, I suppose it is. The children enjoyed putting their pennies into the buckets.'

'So, does your brother work at the hospital, as he was so keen to come along today?'

'No, Percy drives a furniture removal lorry, but his sweetheart is a nurse. She's on one of the floats.'

'Oh, that's interesting.' He raised his brow. 'I'm looking to move to a new house myself, something smaller and safer for my mother. She had a fall on the stairs recently.'

'How terrible. Was she badly hurt?'

'Thankfully not, just bruises, but she's almost eighty, so it could have been so much worse. I can hardly bear to think about it. She's all I've got, you see. I never married. The army was my life, and my men were my family, but those I didn't leave in the mud of France and Belgium froze to death in Murmansk.'

'In Russia? So, you were with the Expeditionary Force in 1919?'

There'd been real pain in his eyes at the mention of his lost men. She knew the campaign to help the White Russians fight the communists had been particularly harsh. Lenny had been glad not to be involved. Poor Edgar must have cared about his men very much.

'Forgive me. You shouldn't have to hear about such things, and I don't want to think about them myself. I gave up my commission after I came home. My mother is my only concern these days. She and I rattle around in our big old house, but it has so many steep stairs. I'm determined to find something better for her. If I ever manage to find somewhere that suits both of us, I might be in need of your brother's services. Does he have a card?'

'No.' She almost laughed at the idea of someone like Percy having a calling card to give out like some rich dandy, although it might actually be a good idea. 'They've only just started out, but they had an advertisement in the *Echo*. The owner is called Frank Scorey, and my brother is Percy Barfoot.'

'These are difficult times for new businesses. I will certainly remember those names, and I promise to look them up and show my support when the time comes.'

When Percy, Lenny and the children came to find her, Laura felt much better. It had been nice to sit in the shade and relax for a while. There was precious little time in her life to rest, and soon enough there'd be even less. The short conversation with Edgar Fielding had been a pleasant distraction. She felt sorry for him to be so worried about his elderly mother and haunted by the men he'd lost in the war. It sounded as if he'd achieved everything Percy had once aspired to, but where had it got him? If his mother was almost eighty, he'd be on his own soon enough, whether he cared to admit it or not. At least she'd never be in that position, and, hopefully, neither would Percy. Ambition and money weren't everything, especially if you had no family to share it with. They might not have much, but they had each other. Maybe another baby might not be as much of a disaster as she thought it would be. They'd manage somehow. They always managed. Even so, she'd keep it to herself a while longer.

40 - Tuesday 13 July 1926

The heat from the bodies packed around Lenny as he came through the dock gate was almost unbearable. He'd been sweating cobs all day while clambering about checking the cargo. Goodness only knew how the poor buggers who had to shift it coped in this muggy weather. Percy was well out of it. He still had to hump furniture around, but at least he had a bit of shade in the cab of the lorry and grateful customers to make him cups of tea. He slung his jacket over his shoulder as he walked past the railings on the edge of the park. The flowers were wilting. They reminded him of Van Gough's yellow roses drooping in a glass. All the moisture was in the air not the ground. He felt as if he was wilting himself. His shirt clung damply to his skin and his hair stuck to his head. He reached the corner of Oxford Street and turned to cross the road. There was old Charlie standing outside the railway station again watching a man unload luggage from a taxicab. His cheeks were carmine red. He must be boiling half to death in that dark uniform topped off with a big helmet.

'Still no sergeant's stripes, then?' he laughed.

'I'm ever hopeful, Lenny, ever hopeful,' Charlie smiled. His face was so red it almost glowed. 'A nice desk job would be just the thing on a day like this. Still, it could be worse. I could be locked up in Winchester gaol waiting for Mr Pierrepoint like Arthur Fisk.'

'I can't say I envy him, even if he did get what he deserves. It's set for August twelfth, isn't it? I don't know why they don't just take them out of the court and do it right off. It seems a bit cruel to make them wait.' If the court case had been a dark cloud hanging over them, what must it be like waiting to be hanged? Of course, Lenny didn't feel sorry for Fisk, but he didn't relish his misery either.

'It's the law. They must have at least three Sundays between the verdict and the drop. It gives them time to make their peace with God, or to appeal.'

'Fisk won't appeal, will he?' Until now, he'd never even considered it. The lifting of the weight of the trial was such a relief for them all; now he could feel it gathering again. He wasn't sure poor Maria could go through all that a second time.

'From what I hear, he already has,' Charlie snorted. A bead of sweat rolled down his cheek and he wiped it away.

'Is there any chance he'll be successful?'

'Not a cat's chance in hell.' Charlie grinned. 'Not unless he's got something up his sleeve. If he has, it'd have to be something bloody good, though.'

Lenny didn't know what to make of this new development. He walked the rest of the way home wondering whether he should even mention it to Laura. The stress of the trial had taken it out of all of them, and she still wasn't her normal self. It was probably best not to worry her with it, but he would tell Percy. A train rattled past. He watched the steam and smoke billowing from its fat little chimney, adding to the water and dirt hanging in the air. Was there even the remotest possibility that Arthur would get off? Charlie didn't seem to think so. Unless he really did have something up his sleeve, but what could he possibly have? The more he thought about it, the more he saw it as nothing more than a desperate man trying to save his neck.

41 - Monday 19 July 1926

Winnie talked a lot. Percy knew some people found that irritating, but he quite liked it. For one thing, it saved him the trouble of thinking of things to say. He also learned lots of interesting things he'd otherwise never have known. Most were about the history of the town, or the history of her family, but she'd also let slip that it was her twenty-seventh birthday this week. He couldn't let such an important day pass unmarked, and, as he and Frank had a quiet morning, he decided to go into town to buy her a gift between jobs. It was Frank who'd suggested he get her a book, something historical, and he recommended a little bookshop in Above Bar. Who'd have thought Frank was a reader. It showed you never could tell about people. He said he was especially fond of a chap called Verne, and another called Wells.

When he got inside the shop, Percy saw he was completely out of his depth. More books than he'd ever seen in his life were packed tightly into every nook and cranny. There were even piles of books on the floor. The whole place had a strange, musty smell. He might have turned round and walked straight back out again if an extremely elderly man with thinning white hair, a bushy moustache and a Gladstone collar hadn't appeared from behind a towering pile of dusty looking tomes and asked if he could help. It was Mr Gilbert, the owner. As it happened, he was very helpful and far sprightlier than he looked, scampering up ladders to reach the highest shelves.

Percy left the shop with a secondhand copy of *Children of the New Forest* tucked in the inside pocket of his jacket. Mr Gilbert called it 'an historic novel,' and said Winnie would love it. Percy didn't know about that, but it certainly looked the part. The green hardback cover even had a picture of cavaliers on horseback. In case she didn't like the book, he dashed up to Maynard's Confectioners. One of the other titbits of information he'd gleaned from Winnie was that she loved wine gums, so he bought her a pocket-sized tin. At least it would prove he'd been listening.

He strolled through the park feeling pretty pleased with himself and much more relaxed than he had for weeks, maybe even months. Fisk, Pothecary and Strange were in gaol, where they belonged. There was no more need for subterfuge and creeping around. Even the news that Fisk was planning an appeal didn't dampen his spirits. His chances of success were slim and, whatever happened, he'd still be locked up. The sun was shining, the parks were green and the sky was clear and blue, just like Winnie's eyes. There was money in his pocket, along with the book and the tin of sweets. What more could a man want?

The bright sunshine bursting through the leaves of the trees ahead made Percy screw up his eyes as he waited to cross the road to Hoglands Park. A tall, thin man in a trench coat and a wide-brimmed fedora was hurrying down Pound Tree Road towards him. He must be baking alive in that get up. A motorcar slowly approached the junction. Percy stopped to let it pass. Then he heard fast footsteps behind him. He spun round. The man in the trench coat was hurtling towards him. As if in slow motion, he took a step to the side to get out of the way. Out of the corner of his eye, he saw the car right beside him. He was caught between the devil and the deep blue sea.

A woman's voice shouted, 'Oi! Watch out.'

The man clattered into Percy hard. The impact winded him and pushed him towards the car. There was no time to think or act. All he could do was struggle to stay on his feet and out of the road. The car stopped with a squeal. The trench coat man pulled away from Percy's grasp. Until that moment, he hadn't realised he'd grabbed hold of him. Then, almost as suddenly as it had started, it was over. The trench coat man flung himself into the car and slammed the door. As it began to pull away, he saw a young woman with a pram at the entrance to the park staring at him. 'Are you all right?' she asked. 'What on earth was the matter with him? I came out of the park and there he was going hell for leather. He almost knocked into my pram and then he almost knocked you into the road. He hasn't robbed you, has he?'

Percy was still trying to regain his breath and slow his pounding heart. He patted his jacket pockets and was relieved to feel coins jangling. Thankfully, the book and the little sweet tin were still there, too.

After a few moments spent reassuring the woman and recovering his composure, Percy carried on across the park towards

St Mary's. What on earth had just happened? He looked around uneasily. A few lads were having a game on the cricket ground with a handful of seagulls as spectators, but the car was long gone. Had it been some kind of accident, like the night he'd almost knocked Winnie down in the dark? Was the man simply rude and in a hurry, or was it something more sinister? It was as if he'd been trying to push him under the wheels of the car. Had Fisk or Pothecary sent someone to get revenge on him? Obviously, it wouldn't be Sam, he wasn't clever enough for that. He tried hard to remember what the man had looked like, but it had been so quick he hadn't seen his face beneath the brim of the hat. Perhaps it really was just a stupid accident; a bad-mannered man in a panic to catch a lift.

42 - Wednesday 21 July 1926

Winnie looked more beautiful than ever this afternoon, in a sea green dress that appeared to be made from layers of gossamer and came just below her knees. Laura would love the long jacket she wore over it. It had a dark blue velvet collar and cuffs and the matching hat was a jaunty little thing with an upturned brim. Unlike Laura, Percy was more interested in the body beneath the clothes, but he had to admit they made her stand out like a rare orchid in a dark forest against the mahogany wainscoting of the café. He smiled at her across the empty teacups and plates on the table between them and fished in his pocket for the book and sweets he'd bought her for her birthday.

'The man in the bookshop said you might like this.' He passed his gifts to her nervously. 'I don't know much about these things, so I hope he was right. Anyway, I know you'll like the sweets. I'm sorry the tin got a bit dented. Some chap ran into me, and they were in my pocket.'

She put the battered tin of sweets down on the table and examined the book with a smile. 'It's just perfect,' she said.

He could tell by the way she stroked the cover and looked inside that she meant it. 'You really didn't have to. The tea and cakes were quite enough.'

'There's just one more thing.' The dark, stained wicker chair creaked as Percy rose and walked around the table to stand at Winnie's side. He took her hand, smiled and got down on one knee. 'Winnie Monk, will you do me the honour—'

'Percy, get up, people are staring,' Winnie hissed. She snatched her hand away and stared angrily down at the table with a face of flaming red.

In that moment, all the hope and happiness flew out of Percy so fast it made his stomach lurch. He got slowly to his feet. A sudden silence had fallen over the café, and the way everyone was looking studiously anywhere but at them made it clear they'd heard it all. She hadn't even let him get the words out. He stood there for a few moments with his hands hanging limply at his sides, frozen to the spot with embarrassment and sadness. He wasn't much of a catch for a woman like Winnie, but he'd really thought she cared for him. Slowly, he turned and went back to his chair. What he really wanted to do was walk away, but he couldn't just leave her there on her own. He'd embarrassed her enough already.

'I'm sorry,' he whispered. 'I thought . . . it doesn't matter. It was stupid of me to think someone like you . . . just forget I said anything.'

43 - Wednesday 21 July 1926

As he strolled along Terminus Terrace in the warm sunshine, Lenny wondered idly what it was like in Guernsey. He'd likely never know, but he imagined it must smell like tomatoes. All morning, he'd been counting crates labelled Guernsey tomatoes. There were thousands of them, and their sweet, earthy scent lingered in his nostrils, at least until he walked a little further and caught the stench of the cattle market. He turned towards the railway bridge, humming a little tune to himself. Unless Laura had put some in tonight's meal, there'd be no more tomatoes until the morning. Wouldn't that be just his luck if she had? Still, it was nice to have nothing better to worry about now all the business with Fisk was over and done with. Even Percy seemed happy and relaxed these days. They probably had Winnie to thank for that.

As he neared the top of the steps, he saw a figure hunched on the wall of the bridge looking down at the rails below. All he could see was the back of his dark brown jacket, but by the size and shape of him, he knew at once it was Percy. He wasn't leaning against the wall but rather sitting on it with his legs dangling towards the track. It was obvious right off that jumping was his aim. No one in his right mind sits on the wall of a railway bridge with their feet dangling over the edge for any other reason. Why, though? He'd been so much happier lately. He had a job, he had Winnie, and he was the hero of the hour after bringing Fisk to justice. He was huddled forwards, with his elbows on his knees and his hands to his temples. Before he even reached him, the stink of beer was overpowering. It was likely Dutch courage. What was he waiting for? Had he changed his mind at the last moment?

He was half afraid to approach in case he startled Percy into jumping. Even without a passing train, the drop onto the rails might do for him. With a sick churning in the pit of his stomach, he crept towards him until he thought he might be able to grab hold of him if he did attempt to jump. Whether he'd be strong enough to haul Percy's struggling bulk back to safety was another matter, but it was as much of a plan as he had.

He leaned against the wall of the bridge and, far more casually than he felt, said, 'That doesn't look like a very comfortable seat, mate.'

He'd expected a fight, or at least a scuffle. His arms were poised ready to grab Percy and pull him backwards. His heart was beating so fast in his ears it felt as if it would burst.

'I missed the fucking train.' Percy turned his head. His eyes were filled with tears, just as they'd been in the trench ten years earlier.

'There'll be no more trains tonight, Percy,' he said. He didn't know if that was true or not. Despite living in a house backing onto the railway line, he hardly ever caught the train and didn't pay much attention to the timetable, but he wasn't going to let Percy jump from the bridge if he could help it. 'Why don't you get down and tell me what's happened?'

'What's happened is that I missed the fucking train.' Percy looked back towards the rails. 'I can't even do that much right. Now you're here to bloody rescue me, as always. Has it ever occurred to you that I don't want to be saved? Just leave me be.'

'So, what shall I tell Laura? "Oh, I saw Percy sitting on the railway bridge, but I just left him there to jump?" What do you think she'd say to that? What about Winnie? What shall I tell her?'

His fear at what Percy might do was fast turning to exasperation. He'd thought all the drinking and self-pity was a thing of the past. What on earth did he have to be miserable about now?

'Winnie?' Percy turned to look at him again. His eyes were half closed and the tears were rolling down his cheeks. 'She'll be glad to be rid of me.'

So, it was about Winnie, then. Had they had a falling out, or was it something worse than that? Perhaps Percy had crossed the line and she'd given him his marching orders? She wasn't Percy's usual tuppenny-ha'penny tart who'd be happy to be manhandled or do the business down a dark alley for a few drinks.

'I thought it was all going well with her?'

'So did I.' Percy wiped his face with the sleeve of his jacket. 'I thought I'd finally found something worth living for, but I was deluded to ever think a woman like her would want someone like me. She didn't even let me finish asking her—'

'Asking her what?'

'To marry me,' he replied, as if it was obvious. 'I should have known better. I really thought she cared for me, but it was a stupid idea.'

'So, she said no, then?'

'Well, she didn't say yes. She wouldn't even let me finish speaking. All she was worried about was people seeing her with me, and who can blame her, eh? Look at me.'

'Let me get this straight.' Lenny's exasperation was fast turning to anger. 'You half asked Winnie to marry you and she didn't say yes, so, now you're going to jump off a bloody bridge? Do you know how many times I asked Laura to marry me?'

'No,' Percy said with a confused frown.

'Three times she said no to me, you stupid sod. Yet never once did I think about trying to top myself. She only said yes in the end because she had Bobby in her belly.'

'Laura said no to you?' Percy looked at him in wonder. 'You never told me.'

'No, because I don't turn everything into a bloody disaster and fill myself with self-pity. I didn't just give up, either. It wasn't as if I was a catch myself, was I? I was still coughing and spluttering from the gas, not knowing if I'd ever get better. I certainly didn't expect her to fall on her knees and be grateful to me for asking. You've only known Winnie a couple of months. She doesn't strike me as the sort of woman who's going to jump into marriage at the drop of a hat.'

Percy had swung one leg back over the bridge and was looking at Lenny in astonishment.

'I've spent all bloody day counting crates of tomatoes and I want to get home, so just get down off there and come with me. And if you breathe one word of this to Laura, I'll drag you back and throw your sorry arse off the bloody bridge myself. Cowards jump off bridges, and she still thinks her brother's a hero. More fool her.'

44 - Thursday 22 July 1926

If the king had been standing on Horseshoe Bridge waiting for her, Laura would have been less surprised. Apart from the trip to Winchester, Maria hadn't left the house for over a year. In fact, it was hard to remember seeing her doing anything other than knitting in Mum's parlour. Now here she was in her summer dress and straw hat as if it was the most normal thing in the world. She looked younger somehow. Perhaps it was because she had a smile on her face.

'To what do I owe this honour?' Laura smiled when Maria took her arm.

'It's such a nice day, I thought I'd get some fresh air and come to meet my little sister.'

'Where's Stanley?' Gladys tugged at Maria's skirt.

'He's helping Granddad in the garden. I think he's hoping you and Bobby will go hunting with him for blackberries.'

'I like blackberries.' Bobby licked his lips. 'Especially when Grandma makes them into jam.'

'And jam tarts,' Gladys said.

'I'm pretty sure Grandma made some this morning,' Maria said.

Now the school holidays were upon them, Laura had to take the children with her everywhere. If they didn't dawdle so, it might have felt less of a chore. She'd pretty much had to drag Bobby away from the log pond near Hetty and Rose's houses. There were a whole group of boys gathered around throwing stones in the water and balancing on the logs nearest the shore. Bobby had looked as if he wanted to join them. Goodness only knew what he and Gladys got up to when she wasn't around. Hopefully, they kept well away from the river. One mention of jam tarts, though, and they were skipping off along the road at top speed.

'No further than the level crossing,' Laura shouted after them. Then she turned to Maria. 'It's good to see you out of the house.'

They might not always get along, but she meant it.

'It's good to be outside and see all this.' Maria waved her hand to indicate the little gardens with roses blooming, the groups of children playing in the street and the postman slowly going from house to house. 'Now that Fisk is in gaol and due to hang, I don't have to look at every man who passes and wonder if he was the one who killed my Fred. It got to the point where I couldn't face going outside at all. Then it was as if I were in prison, but now, thanks to Percy, I've been set free.'

'He does have his uses sometimes.'

She'd known Maria was unhappy, but all the sitting in the

parlour knitting had seemed like a choice. If she'd realised how trapped her sister felt she might have tried to force her to go out, or at least visited her more often.

'I can't even begin to say how grateful I am to him. He risked a lot to bring that horrible man to justice.'

'Maybe you should tell him that.'

'I did try when we were in Winchester, but he seemed a bit embarrassed by it. He's never been one for people making a fuss over him, has he? Even when he was a little boy, he'd wipe off kisses and shrug off hugs.'

'You should try again. Not the kisses and hugs, of course, just telling him how much what he did meant to you. He could do with cheering up right now.'

'Why? I thought things were looking up for him. He's not lost that job, has he?'

'No, that's going quite well. They've got a regular thing with a couple of furniture makers in town now, making deliveries for them. He's had a falling out with Winnie, though.'

'Don't tell me he's overstepped the mark. She didn't sound like the sort of woman who'd put up with any nonsense.' Maria pulled a face that said exactly what kind of nonsense she meant.

'No, it was nothing like that,' Laura laughed. 'As far as I can tell, he's been the perfect gentleman. Actually, he asked her to marry him yesterday afternoon, or so Lenny told me.'

'But they hardly know each other.'

'Well, you know what Percy's like. Once he gets an idea in his head, he goes steaming ahead without a thought. Look at what he was like with the army. As soon as he decided that was what he wanted to do, he was off to join the territorials, even though he was barely old enough. He throws himself in at the deep end with no thought for the consequences and then acts like it's the end of the world when it all goes wrong.'

'I assume she said no?'

'And he was surprised.' Laura shook her head sadly. 'If he'd asked me, I'd have told him. It's too soon for a start. No woman wants to be rushed into marriage these days. Besides, she's an ambitious type. She told me she wants to become matron one day. She'd have to give up those ideas if she married.'

'Poor Percy, it sounds like he's lovestruck. I never thought I'd see the day.'

'Well, now he's moping around the place. He was as drunk as a lord when he came home last night, and he didn't go out again to walk her home from work, even though it was her birthday.'

'So, he's sulking?'

'Yes, but don't tell Mum. I think she was hoping he'd finally started to settle down.'

They'd reached the level crossing now. Bobby and Gladys were hopping from foot to foot waiting for them. Laura took their hands, and they crossed the railway line. Every journey she made seemed to involve crossing and re-crossing the bloody railway lines. Just on the short walk to Mum's house, they had to negotiate the gasworks spur crossing their road, another on Britannia Road, then the little single track that ran past the log pond to the wharf, the crossing at Mount Pleasant, Horseshoe Bridge, and the level crossing on Adelaide Road. Sometimes, she wished she could get away from the railway altogether. Still, they'd be at Mum's in another few minutes. Hopefully, Maria would keep quiet about Percy and Winnie. Keeping secrets from her was becoming a habit these days.

45 - Saturday 24 July 1926

Bobby and Gladys had left Laura at the end of the road and joined a group of local children playing a game that involved flicking cigarette cards at a wall. Whenever Percy opened a new packet of cigarettes, they begged him for the cards inside. Maybe this was why. Laura carried on alone with her basket on her arm and her head full of the jobs she had to do. One of Rose's friends wanted some pinafores made, and she had the cloth and thread for them in her basket, along with a chicken for the Sunday roast. It was a little cooler today, which felt like a blessing. Then she saw someone standing on her doorstep, a very small someone in a pale blue dress and dark blue jacket. What on earth was Winnie doing calling on her? Of course, she was probably calling on Percy, but he and Frank had left at first light for a big moving job somewhere in Swaythling.

'Percy's not due back for ages,' she said as she fished her key out of her pocket. 'But you're welcome to come in if you want.'

Truth to tell, she half hoped Winnie would decline and leave her to get on with her work. She was curious to hear her side of the marriage proposal story, but the house was in its usual mess, and she'd left dirty dishes in the sink. The place was bad enough when it was tidy, and Winnie was so grand.

'That would be nice, as long as I won't be in your way.' Winnie smiled, but there was a hint of nervousness beneath it.

'As long as you don't mind the state of the place. I wasn't set up for guests.' Laura opened the door and waved Winnie inside. 'Why don't you go and sit in the parlour while I put this chicken in the meat safe and get the kettle on?'

'Why don't I put the kettle on while you put the meat away?' Winnie bypassed the parlour door and followed her into the kitchen. 'I might not be much of a cook, but I do know how to work a range, and I'm not worried by a little mess. Nursing isn't all wiping fevered brows, you know. I spend half my life up to my armpits in filth of every kind.'

Before Laura had a chance to stop her, Winnie had filled the kettle and put it on the hob.

'Don't look so uncomfortable,' she said when Laura came back from the meat safe and found her with her sleeves rolled up rinsing the dishes in the sink. 'This house reminds me of the one we used to live in in London, except ours had a hole in the roof and water poured in whenever it rained.'

'So did ours, until Percy climbed up in the attic and fixed it,' Laura laughed. Perhaps Winnie wasn't quite as grand as she looked.

'There's no shame in it. This is far tidier than ours was, and my mum only had one child making a mess. Believe me, though, I was a messy child.' The kettle began to whistle. 'Why don't you fill the teapot and pour some hot water in this sink, then I'll wash these dishes for you?'

'There's no need for that.'

'Nonsense. You look like you've been on the go all day. It can't be easy running around after two men and two children, especially as you've got another on the way, if I'm not mistaken.'

'How did you know?' Laura was horrified. Was it so obvious? If it was, how long before Lenny or Percy worked it out?

'I'm a nurse.' Winnie smiled and shook her head. 'I'm not sure why everyone keeps forgetting that. Actually, I've just started a midwifery course. We've been learning all about the butterfly pigmentation pregnant women get, and I can see it in your face.'

'Please keep it to yourself. What with everything that's been going on, and Arthur Fisk's appeal, I haven't told anyone yet.'

'Don't worry, your secret's safe with me. Now, pour some water into this sink.'

Once the tea was brewed and the washing up done, they went to sit in comfort in the parlour. Winnie wittered on about her plans to train as a midwife. 'There's quite some money to be made, and it's a bit more of an adventure than being stuck in the hospital with the sister breathing down my neck.'

It was a dismal day, almost chilly. Laura let Winnie's chatter wash over her and looked at the empty grate. Maybe she should build a fire. It seemed like an extravagant waste of coal, though, when she could just wrap a shawl around her shoulders.

'So, how's Percy?' Winnie took a sip of her tea and didn't meet Laura's eye. She'd finally got round to the real reason for her visit. All the earlier blustering and talk about her childhood and learning to be a midwife was nothing but waffle.

'Moping about, mostly.' Laura let out a long, slow breath. She didn't want to fall out with Winnie, but she had to say something. 'He may act like the big tough man, but he's actually quite fragile underneath all the bravado. He went through a terrible time after he got wounded. It's not just his face. He broke his leg so badly he almost lost it. The bone of his thigh was sticking out through his skin.'

'I know.' Winnie nodded sadly.

'He told you?' Percy never usually told anyone about the wounds you couldn't see.

'Not me as such. On the day we met, he told the young lad with the crushed leg about it. He was trying to help him keep calm and let him know it wasn't the end of the world. I just overheard, but he has told me a little more since then.'

'Well, it was the end of Percy's world in a way. It was the end of all the ambitions he had. He was never the same afterwards, and his face is a constant reminder. People look at him in the street, you know. Children are afraid of him, and women, well, he has no luck with them.'

'But he has you and Lenny, and your children.'

'He thought he had you, too.' Laura looked Winnie in the eye. 'Now it seems he doesn't. So, why have you come here? It isn't to tell me about learning to deliver babies, or to do my washing up, is it?'

'Because I care about him.' Winnie held Laura's gaze. 'Even on that first day, there was something about him. He was so kind and gentle with that lad and yet he looked so big and rough and . . . and I couldn't stop thinking about him. When he bumped into me in the dark, it was as if he'd appeared by magic. Then he started appearing every night, like a big, brutish-looking guardian angel.'

'And then he asked you to marry him, or at least tried to.' Laura raised an eyebrow. 'And the thought of spending your life with someone like him suddenly wasn't very appealing.'

'I didn't handle it very well.' Winnie looked at her feet. 'It was so unexpected. We only met in May. It's too soon to talk about marriage. I have my own ambitions, and weddings and children have never been among them.'

'I gathered that, and I understand. But Percy is, well, he's Percy. When he's set his sights on something, he just ploughs on ahead without a thought. Since he met you, I've never seen him so happy, and now I've hardly seen him so sad.'

'The last thing I wanted was to hurt him, and I know I have hurt him. When he stopped coming to meet me, I realised that although I might not be ready for marriage, I'm not ready to lose him, either.'

'Then you need to tell him.'

46 - Wednesday 28 July 1926

Percy pulled on his cigarette and willed the hands on the clock to move so he could leave to meet Winnie after work. On Saturday afternoon, when he found her and Laura giggling in the parlour over tales of his childhood, his heart had felt as if it would burst with happiness. Ever the diplomat, Laura left them alone for a long talk. Now he saw he'd been too hasty, rushing from courting to marriage at top speed without thinking about what Winnie wanted.

He glanced across at Laura, who had her head bent over her knitting. She'd always said he was too impulsive and should count to ten before he rushed into things. She said a lot of sensible things. He should probably listen to her more often. After all, she'd said no to Lenny three times. He still couldn't quite believe he hadn't known about that. Looking at him now, dozing in the chair beside Laura with his mouth open catching flies, he could see her point. At least Winnie still cared for him, and he hadn't completely ruined it. He'd have to take a leaf out of Lenny's book, bide his time and ask her again in a few months.

There was a rapping at the door. Percy got up to answer and was surprised to find Charlie West on the doorstep.

'You'll be getting us a bad reputation with the neighbours, turning up in your uniform in the dead of night.' Percy chuckled and waved him inside. It was beginning to rain again. Hopefully, it wouldn't be as bad as Monday night, when he and Winnie could easily have rowed a boat home.

'I've come with good news and a strange request.' Charlie took off his helmet, ran his hand through his sparse hair and stepped over the threshold. 'Sorry it's so late, but it's not strictly official police business and I've just come off duty.'

'You'd better come in, then.' Percy led Charlie through to the parlour.

Laura put down her knitting and shot a quizzical look at Charlie as he stepped into the room. Lenny rubbed his eyes. Percy pointed at the chair he'd left to answer the door. His cigarette was still burning in the ashtray on the arm. 'Have a seat, Charlie.'

'Can I make you a cup of tea?' Laura put her hands on the arms of her chair as if to rise.

'Thanks for the offer, but I won't stop because the wife will have my pie in the oven. It's always beef on Wednesdays. I do like a nice beef pie.' He patted his stomach. The silver buttons straining on his tunic were testament to his love of pies of all kinds. 'I just wanted to be the one to tell you the news.'

'Let me guess, Fisk's appeal has been declined?' Lenny sat up in the chair, yawned and stretched.

'Yes, the judges threw it out, just as I knew they would. It was all a load of hogwash, as far as I can tell. He admitted he'd robbed the bakery that night and that he took the money from the cash box, but he says he ran off when he heard Fred opening the door from the kitchen and never touched him.'

'So, who did, then? A ghost? Or is he saying Fred bashed himself over the head?' Percy plopped into his chair, picked up his cigarette and took a drag. It was the most ridiculous story he'd heard. If anything, it made Fisk look guiltier.

'He says he had accomplices, but he won't name them.' Charlie raised his eyebrows. It was clear he didn't believe it. 'Admitting he robbed the place was never going to help him unless he was willing to point the finger at someone else, or someone else grew a conscience and confessed.'

'Could he really have had accomplices, or is he just clutching at straws?' Lenny asked.

'Your guess is as good as mine.' Charlie shrugged his huge shoulders. 'But I doubt it. After all, his were the only fingerprints found. He'd have been better off naming the others at his trial, if there really were any others. If the jury believed there was more than one possible culprit and couldn't decide which one had done it, there might have been reasonable doubt. Instead, he thought he could just deny everything, stand there smiling and get away with murder. I'm sure it was that smile the jury took exception to.'

'If there really were accomplices, though, and one of them killed Fred, why wouldn't he name them?' Laura asked. 'They're hardly worth protecting if they're willing to let him hang.'

'Loyalty, fear, who knows?' Charlie stuck out his bottom lip. 'Or maybe it was all just another lie he thought they'd believe. He was trying to save his neck, remember.'

'Well, it didn't work, did it?' Percy smiled. 'So, that's that, then. Now, what was this other thing you mentioned? You said it was something strange?'

'In more ways than one,' Charlie chuckled. 'I had a telephone call from one of the prison guards not long after I learned the appeal had been dismissed. Sam Strange is desperate to speak to you, Percy. He says it's a matter of life and death and he doesn't trust anyone else. Whether it's anything to do with the case or some weird and wonderful figment of his imagination, I couldn't say. I do know he's been weeping and wailing because his mother hasn't been to see him, so it's likely to be something to do with that.'

'Does he seriously still believe she's his mother?' Lenny asked.

'Absolutely. He's been writing to her every day, and the guard said he's devastated she hasn't replied or visited. He's quite lost his mind over it. He honestly thought she'd be at the trial to hold his hand. My guess is he wants Percy to talk to her. He'll have a job, though. She disappeared right after she sold all his possessions. By now, she's probably found another poor idiot to con.'

'That's quite sad,' Laura winced. 'I almost feel sorry for him.'

47 - Monday 2 August 1926

If it hadn't been for Laura, Percy might not have bothered to go and see Sam. After all, he didn't owe him anything, even if he did feel a little sorry for him. Of all of them, Sam was the least culpable. Left to his own devices, he'd never have got involved in robberies or anything of that kind. The lad could barely read and write, never mind mastermind a criminal gang. Percy wanted to put the whole thing behind him, though. Even Maria's gratitude was embarrassing. He wasn't a hero. He'd done nothing brave. He'd simply been in the right place at the right time and put two and two together. Now he had Winnie and work to think about. There weren't enough hours in the day to get involved in looking for Sam's mother, especially as it was highly unlikely she was who she claimed to be, and finding her would bring Sam more grief than happiness.

Laura saw it differently. 'I can't stop thinking about that poor boy all alone in gaol and abandoned by the woman he thinks is his mother,' she said when he told her he wasn't going to go. 'I know he's an idiot, but he's a harmless idiot. The least you could do is listen to him. Maybe you could make him see sense, or at least let him down gently. Otherwise, he's just going to keep on pining. Besides, aren't you just a teeny bit curious about what he thinks is so important, and why he'll only talk to you?'

So, against his better judgement, here he was in a small, bare room with a barred window so high in the wall it might as well have not been there. Percy sat on the hard chair close to the narrow bed. The door wasn't locked and there was a guard outside, but the claustrophobia was palpable, even in the few minutes he'd been there. Sam looked dreadful. His freckly face was pale and gaunt, with long red scratches down his cheeks and stubble on his chin. His hair was wild, but not as wild as his eyes. The guard said they'd put him in the straitjacket to stop him tearing his hair out and scratching his face. Now he couldn't even move his arms. It was piteous.

'You've got to help me, Percy.' Both his eyes darted in different directions in a disconcerting way. 'I can't trust anyone in here. There are spies everywhere. They watch me all the time. They know I won't let it go. I can't let it go.'

He was rambling like a lunatic. He really had lost his mind. Despite everything, Percy was sad to see him come to this.

'Is it your mother you want to see me about, Sam?' he asked kindly. If he could just get him to calm down, he might get some sense out of him.

'My mother?' Sam frowned, as if he were trying to remember what the word meant. 'Jimmy said she weren't my mother at all. He said I was a fool to believe her. Maybe I was, but I wanted a mother so bad, and she looked after me, she really did. Why shouldn't she be my mother? She said her baby was taken from his pram and she knew I was him. She said she'd know me anywhere because she loved me so much. Nobody ever loved me before. It weren't hurting nobody, her being my mother, so why should Jimmy try to stop her?'

'Of course it wasn't hurting anyone, Sam. As long as she made you happy.'

'She did make me happy.' Sam stuck out his bottom lip like a child. 'Jimmy didn't like it, though. He didn't have no mother, either, and he didn't want me to have one. At least he remembered his mother. He could remember what her face was like, leastwise, before his father beat it in. You know he saw his father beating her? He says he tried to stop him. He hit him over the head with the flat iron, but it was too late. She was already dead. Then they hanged his father and he ended up in the workhouse, just like me. He had a mother and a father for ten years, though. That was ten years more than I ever had.'

'So, do you want me to speak to your mother? Is that why you wanted to see me?'

'No.' Sam looked at him as if he was the one who'd gone mad. 'Ma had nothing to do with it. She don't know nothing, and don't you let anyone tell you she does. It's about the other thing.' Sam looked towards the door suspiciously.

'What other thing, Sam? If it's not about your mother, then what is it about?'

'I need to get out of here, Percy. If he finds out I've talked to you he's going to do for me. I can't let it go, though. I just can't. It ain't right.'

'Sam, I can't get you out of here. No one can. If that's why you asked me to come, you are wasting your time, and mine.'

Percy was losing patience with Sam's rambling. Nothing he said made sense. He'd come all this way with Frank and given up a bank holiday he could have been spending with Winnie, all to listen to the ravings of a mad man.

'But he'll kill me.' Sam began to cry, and he rocked back and forth wildly. 'Just like he did that baker.'

'Arthur? You think Arthur is going to kill you for speaking to me? Why would he do that? They're going to hang him no matter what anyone says.'

'Not Arthur.' He leaned forward and whispered, 'Jimmy. They're going to hang Arthur, but it was Jimmy that did it. I saw him. You have to stop them, Percy.'

Percy reeled out of the oppressive little room and into the corridor, with its rows of doors, chequered floor and metal stairs. The walkways above, supported by arched metal brackets, pressed in on him. The weight of all the incarcerated men, the smell of their fear and their misery made him want to run screaming from the place. No wonder Sam had lost his mind at the prospect of being stuck in there for five years.

'What did he want that was so urgent?' the guard sneered.

'He wanted me to find his mother and look after her,' Percy lied. Sam might be half mad, but it was fear that had made him that way, and it seemed he had good reason to be afraid.

Outside the prison walls, he gasped for air. He looked back at the towering red brick monstrosity, all mean little windows that let in no light, and shuddered. Then he ran, as fast as his legs would carry him, past the long wall topped by tall trees and the houses opposite, with their elegant porticoed doors and basement railings in stark contrast to their neighbour. He kept running until he was no longer hemmed in by those dark walls and could see the flint and stone of the court building, the shrunken Bargate arch and Bert's motorcar. Frank was standing beside it nonchalantly smoking a cigarette. 'You look like you need a drink,' he grinned when Percy, panting for breath, came to a halt in front of him.

'There's no time for drinking, Frank,' he gasped. 'We have to find Charlie West. There are lives at stake, and he'll know what to do.'

48 - Saturday 7 August 1926

The Bell and Crown was packed, as it always was on a Saturday night, but they'd managed to find a table near the window. Lenny could hear Gladys's voice outside; she was yelling at Bobby. Someone was playing a mournful tune on the old piano. Lenny didn't recognise it, but it jarred with the celebratory mood of their little group. In five short days, so much had changed. He looked around the table. Charlie now had his sergeant's stripes, although he was out of uniform tonight. He looked smaller somehow. Percy was a hero twice over for saving Arthur's neck and bringing Jimmy to justice. Laura was pregnant and, to his mind, it was the best news this horrible year had brought.

He couldn't stop grinning about it. She'd kept it from him because she was worried about money and how they'd fit another body into their cramped little house. He didn't care about any of that. He'd been thinking about finding another house for ages. He wanted to get away from these filthy streets, and now he might just have a chance. Frank was talking about getting another lorry because he and Percy had more work on than they could manage between them. Percy was going to teach him to drive so he could leave the docks behind. It was easy, according to Percy, much easier than driving a cart with a horse that might decide to bolt or stop at any time.

He looked across the table. Percy was laughing his head off at some joke he and Charlie had shared while he wasn't listening.

'So, this copper was peddling like mad on his bicycle, but he couldn't catch us,' Percy chortled. 'I never knew a motorcar could go so fast, but Frank must have had his foot to the floor.'

'It'll be a different story when the constabulary are given motor vehicles.' Charlie gave Percy a mock stern look. 'Then people won't be able to drive like madmen without being caught. I hear they're looking at getting a motorcycle. It's top of the range and very fast. Frank will have to watch his heavy foot then.'

'They'd have needed an aeroplane to catch Frank that day,' Percy said. 'We lost the copper on the Twyford Road, and then, when we got back here, we had the devil's own job finding you, Charlie. We were driving round in a panic for what felt like hours. Frank kept saying, "Bloody coppers everywhere when you're up to no good, but as soon as you want one, they're nowhere to be found." Your cars must have been burning.'

'What I don't understand,' Lenny said. 'Is why Arthur kept his mouth shut? Why would he be willing to swing for Jimmy?'

'When he gave his statement, he said that at first, he thought Sam had killed Fred.' Charlie took a swig from his pint. 'What he said about running off with the money from the cash box was true. Jimmy and Sam weren't as quick as he was, and they got caught in the shop. Afterwards, Jimmy told him Sam had bashed Fred over the head. Sam was in a terrible state and wouldn't say anything at all, so he believed it. He only worked out the truth when Jimmy attacked Mr Petheridge. When he confronted him, Jimmy admitted it, but Arthur couldn't turn him in or he'd implicate himself, and Jimmy said he'd kill Arthur's mother and sister if he told anyone. It was them he was trying to save by going to the gallows.'

Lenny looked at Laura sipping her stout with a white moustache of froth on her upper lip. In the same position, he could see himself going to the gallows to keep her and the children safe, but it still didn't quite make sense.

'But once they were all in prison, Jimmy couldn't hurt Arthur's family. So, why didn't he speak up then?'

'Arthur says Jimmy has some very scary friends on the outside who are more than willing to do his bidding,' Charlie said. 'Sam said the same. He knew all along what Jimmy had done. He saw him do it. Jimmy threatened to have his mother killed if he opened his mouth, and he believed him.'

'So, that was what sent him mad, then?' Laura put her glass down on the table. 'He thought Jimmy was going to have his mother killed? Even though she's not really his mother at all?'

'Actually, young Sam turned out to be a lot brighter than we thought,' Charlie said. 'Once he knew she might be in danger, he told his mother, or whatever she is, to sell everything in the house and disappear, and it looks like she did just that. I've an idea he knows exactly where she is, though.'

'So, he knew she was safe all along?' Percy screwed up his face in disbelief. 'That makes no sense. Why was he ranting and raving about her and sending her letters if he knew she was safe? I saw him in that cell, and he was off his trolley. They had him in a straitjacket.'

'It was the only way he could be sure *he* was safe himself.' Charlie's eyebrows curled at the irony. 'He realised they'd lock him away from the other prisoners, including Jimmy, if he could make them think he'd lost his mind. That's why he made such a fuss about his mother and kept sending her letters. The lad can hardly read or write after all. Plus, it was a good way to get to see you, Percy. He convinced them the only way he'd stop trying to hurt himself and calm down was to let you visit him. You were the only person he felt he could trust to do the right thing.'

'Do you think Jimmy really does have someone on the outside to do his bidding?' Lenny didn't like the sound of that very much. If he did, wouldn't they be after Percy now? Right when he finally thought he could stop worrying about him, too.

'I doubt it,' Charlie said. 'If he had, I'm pretty sure they'd have tried to take revenge on Percy here by now. I think he was manipulating the pair of them. For all Arthur Fisk's arrogance, he did exactly what Jimmy told him to do. It was Sam, the one he trusted the most and feared the least, who bettered him in the end.'

49 - Thursday 12 August 1926

Laura leaned back in the deckchair and tilted her head to the sun. It was good to feel the warmth on her face and inhale the earthy smells of summer, the overblown roses and freshly cut grass. She rested her hand on her tight stomach and felt the butterfly fluttering inside her. At least she didn't have to hide it any more. Not that hiding it had been all that successful in some quarters.

When she confessed, Mum had merely smiled and said, 'I wondered when you were going to tell me,' and Maria had already knitted a new nursing shawl.

The murmur of the children talking as they helped Granddad weed the vegetable plot drifted across the garden. She opened her eyes and glanced lazily across at them. Gladys was sprawled on her belly, swinging her long, sun browned legs, and carefully teasing the weeds from the soil. Bobby knelt beside her, his blonde head bowed in concentration. A little way off, Stanley, smaller and paler than both of them, had filled a trug with a pile of chickweed and sat back on his heels. It was strange to think of the child growing inside her one day doing the same. Who would it look like? Would it be another Gladys, loud and obstreperous, or like Bobby, quiet and thoughtful?

Dad leaned on his hoe and smiled at her. His corduroy trousers were patched at the knee, his shirt sleeves were rolled up and his moth eaten waistcoat had begun to unravel here and there. He had a battered old cap on his head protecting his bald pate from the sun and his twinkling eyes were full of mirth and love in a sea of leathery wrinkles. Had he ever been a boy like Bobby? It seemed impossible, yet he must have been. While she could remember Mum younger and slimmer with dark hair, Dad had always been the same, although he might have once had more than the few tufts of white fuzz sticking out from under his cap.

'They'd have hanged that Fisk chap today if it hadn't been for Percy,' Maria said. She and mum had been chewing over the whys and wherefores of the recent revelations, but Laura had stopped paying attention.

'I still don't understand what's going to happen now,' Mum said. 'Will Jimmy Pothecary hang now, or will they have to have another trial?'

'And the Fisk Chap, what will happen to him?' Maria said.

'I'm not sure how it works,' Laura finally joined the conversation. She was the only one of them who'd heard from the horse's mouth after all. 'Charlie said the judges have listened to Sam and Arthur's statements and overturned Arthur's murder conviction. I suppose that means he will serve the seven years Jimmy would have.'

'And Pothecary will hang?' Maria looked anxious.

'I suppose so.' Laura rubbed her belly thoughtfully, 'Just not today. When he realised he couldn't get out of it he confessed, or so Charlie says. I don't suppose they need another trial after that. They've moved him to Pentonville so he can't do anything to Arthur and Sam. His father hanged too you know. Perhaps it was in his blood all along.'

While Mum and Maria carried on deliberating on all the ins and outs of it, Laura closed her eyes and tuned them out again. She tried to return to thinking about the baby growing inside her but Jimmy's story wouldn't quite go away. What turned a man like him into a murderer? Had seeing his father kill his mother made him blasé about violence and murder, or was it really something inside him all the time? Could a person be born evil or did the world around them turn them that way? If it really was in the blood, what was in her blood, or Percy's, Lizzie's, Ethel's, Maria's and Willy's. All six of them were very different but they all had bits of Mum and Dad mixed up inside them, just as Gladys and Bobby had bits of her and Lenny. Could any of them have done what Jimmy did if life had dealt them a different hand? She hoped not, but it was a frightening thought all the same.

50 - Saturday 18 September 1926

As he climbed the steps of the railway bridge, Percy tried to exorcise the memory of looking down at the rails waiting for a train to come and end his misery. He'd been a fool, and if it weren't for Lenny, he'd be a dead fool. Then Arthur might have hanged for a crime he didn't commit, and Jimmy would still be sitting in prison laughing because he'd managed to get away with murder. Yesterday, when Charlie came to tell him they'd hanged him, it felt like justice had finally been done. If he'd jumped, he'd have missed this expanse of blue sky, the leaves changing colour on the trees and drifting in the breeze, and the happiness bursting out of his heart.

Winnie had finally done what Laura and Lenny had been trying to do for years. She'd made him realise life was worth living. It hadn't ended with a shell in No Man's Land after all. She said she was proud he'd fought for his country, and that his wounds were badges of honour, not shame. For ten long years, Laura had been telling him he was wasting his life with all the bitter regrets and self-pity, but it was Winnie who'd made him believe it. Now she'd agreed to marry him, so he knew for sure he was one of the lucky ones. If she was willing to give up her aspirations for him, then he could finally stop mourning his own.

He had a spring in his step as he crossed the bridge. Once he'd dealt with Mr Fielding, he'd meet Lenny and take him to see the house he'd found. It was a little further from the docks, but Lenny wouldn't have to worry about that soon. Bert was fixing up a second lorry for Frank and, in a week or two, it would all be up and running so Lenny could drive it, with Bert's stepson, George, helping lump the furniture. He was a small lad, just out of school, but strong and willing. The pair of them would be like David and Goliath.

As soon as he saw the house, he knew it was perfect for Laura and Lenny. It was another terrace, but it had three bedrooms and a privy right by the back door, not to mention a nice little garden with no trainline at the bottom of it. Laura wouldn't know herself. As soon as they'd finished moving Mrs Mobley out, he'd spoken to the landlord and the place was theirs if they wanted it. The rent was higher but not so high he and Lenny wouldn't be able to manage it, and by the time he and Winnie were married, Lenny would be earning more from Frank anyway. He couldn't wait to see Lenny's face when he saw the place, but first he had to see what Mr Fielding wanted moving. Bert's wife, Hetty, took all their telephone calls and she'd been a bit vague about this one. She said he was a military chap turned furniture restorer, and he'd asked for Percy specifically. If he played his cards right, it might turn into another regular job.

51 - Saturday 18 September 1926

Another working week was over and, with five shiploads of French fruit arriving almost every day, Lenny had had his work cut out. With any luck, there wouldn't be too many more weeks like it. Every evening this month, he'd been practising driving Frank's lorry under Percy's supervision. It was pretty easy once he'd got the hang of the size of the thing. That's what Laura thought they were doing tonight, but actually they were going to look at a house Percy had found. He'd been keeping his eyes peeled since discovering Laura was pregnant again, and when he and Frank had moved the tenant out of this one, he'd known it was perfect for them.

It certainly sounded good, especially the privy. Winter would soon be upon them and walking down to the bottom of the yard to use the toilet in the ice and snow was not an appealing thought. They'd all had a tough year, what with the strike and all the business with Fisk and Pothecary, but maybe things were finally beginning to look up. Of course, he had to see the place first. There was no point getting Laura's hopes up if it turned out to have half a roof and rotten windows, or the stench of a glue factory or worse wafting over it. You never could tell with Percy.

He strolled along Terminus Terrace in high spirits, enjoying the early evening sun. For once, there was no hurry. Percy was meeting a chap in one of the arches behind the cattle market. He'd called him a prospective client. Imagine Percy using words like that. He said the chap restored old furniture and was looking for a company to move it around. Somehow, he'd got hold of Percy's name. Maybe Laura's idea to have cards printed to hand out to people they met had paid off. Percy didn't know how long the meeting would take, but he said he'd find him in the Bristol Hotel when it was over and then they'd go and see the house.

A few fallen leaves fluttered along the street like flakes of gold, forming little eddies at his feet. The year was turning and the nights were slowly drawing in. Hopefully, Percy wouldn't get chatting, at least not for too long. He'd like to see the new house in daylight, and he was famished. He crossed Oxford Street and, with a twinge of guilt, passed the London Hotel where he'd seen Percy with Fisk and Pothecary back in the summer. How could he have thought Percy would be involved in their shenanigans?

The street was quiet. It was a little early yet for the pubs to fill up. Ahead, he saw Percy outside the arches talking to a couple of men. He was too far away to see any of them clearly, but Percy was easily recognisable in his Sunday suit, all set to impress. One of the men leaned forward and opened the door of the arch opposite the Bristol Hotel. He went inside, followed by Percy and the second man. Lots of small businesses used the arches under the steeply sloping road to the bridge. He'd never seen inside any of them and was quite curious to know what they were like, but by the time he got to the Bristol Hotel, the door was closed. Maybe if they got the contract, he'd be able to satisfy his curiosity another time.

LAND FIT FOR HEROES

52 - Saturday 18 September 1926

When Percy turned the corner, two men in dark suits and trilby hats were waiting outside the door of the arches. They looked like toffs, so he was glad he'd worn his Sunday suit. He wondered if he should get himself a trilby to replace his old cap. As he approached the men, he arranged his face into what he hoped was a pleasant smile. With any luck, this wouldn't take too long. He wanted to get Lenny to the new house before it got dark.

'Mr Fielding?' he held out his hand.

'Actually, Mr Fielding is inside.' The shorter of the two men shook his hand. He had a military bearing and a bushy moustache. 'I'm Mr Burr and this is Mr Perkins. We're his associates.'

Mr Perkins was tall, thin and clean-shaven. While Percy shook his hand, Mr Burr opened the door. Percy followed him inside with Mr Perkins bringing up the rear. 'Mind the steps,' he said.

There were three stone steps. Once he'd reached the bottom, the first thing he noticed was the darkness, especially when Mr Perkins closed the door behind him. There was a Tilley lamp on a table at the back of the place, but the light it cast did little to illuminate the gloom. Perhaps they had no electricity here, lots of places hadn't, but he'd have thought it would be better to hang the lamp from the ceiling. The place was much smaller than he'd expected, too. It was more of a cavern or a cellar than a warehouse, with a low vaulted ceiling of rough brick curving to the floor. It put him in mind of some of the better dugouts in France, or the cellars they'd been billeted in.

He glanced around. Two men were huddled in the darkest corner at the far side of the room. One of them must be Mr Fielding, but it was so dark he couldn't see either of their faces. The place was bare apart from the table the lamp was on and a wooden chair pushed against the back wall. Where was all the furniture being repaired? Where was the smell of wood shavings and wax polish? All he could smell was damp brick. Something about this wasn't right. A twinge of alarm shot through him. His mind ran at a mile a minute. He thought about Jimmy Pothecary and his dangerous friends. He'd got used to being on his guard after Sam told him about Jimmy's threats, but now the murderer had been hanged, he'd stopped worrying. Maybe he'd relaxed too soon.

The men in the corner stepped towards the light. Percy's heart felt as if it had stopped when he recognised the fascist from the Bell and Crown at the beginning of May and the monkey man who'd been with him. He clenched his fists and tried to swing but the two men behind him grabbed his arms. He struggled and kicked out wildly as he tried to wrench his arms free. A few of the kicks made contact but he couldn't free his arms. Now the fascist was right in front of him, and monkey man had joined his captors, so he had three men hanging off his arms trying to subdue him. Then the fascist pulled a revolver from his pocket and pointed it at Percy. He stopped struggling and stared at the gun. He recognised it at once; it was a service revolver, a Webley.

'Ah, Percy, we finally meet again,' the fascist sneered. In the dim light, he looked almost satanic, with a long, narrow face and his small eyes in shadow under his jutting brow. 'You've led my associates quite a merry dance since we last met. Either you are far cleverer than I gave you credit for, and you knew they were following you, or you have extraordinarily good luck. You even managed to escape when Mr Perkins here tried to get you into my motorcar.'

The image of the dented sweet tin popped into Percy's head. So, Perkins was the trench coat man who'd almost knocked him under the wheels of a car back in July. He'd dismissed it as a figment of his imagination. How many other things had he dismissed when he should have been paying attention?

The three men dragged him to the chair and, with the gun still pointed at him, tied his hands behind his back and wrapped the rope round his chest, anchoring him fast.

'Forgive me for being so rude, Percy,' the fascist smirked. 'I haven't introduced myself properly. My name is Captain Edgar Fielding.' Then he turned to the other men, as if he was dismissing servants. 'Pitt, Burr, Perkins, thank you for your services, you may leave now. Give me half an hour then bring the car for me.'

'What do you want with me?' Percy said once the men had

gone.

'Well, when we last met, you made rather a fool of me in front of my associates. I'm not fond of being made to look a fool, especially by a common Tommy like you. You made a mistake, Percy, you struck a superior officer. And not only that, you had your lackeys cover me in beer and dump me outside the police station like rubbish. Do you know what the penalty for striking a superior officer is?' He arched one eyebrow. 'It's death.'

'So, call the military police and court-martial me, then. I haven't been in the army since nineteen-sixteen, so I doubt you'll have much luck with that.'

He had to keep Fielding talking while he worked out how to get out of this. There had to be a way. He thought of Winnie and her big blue eyes. He hadn't finally got everything he wanted in life for it to end like this.

'Oh, I think we can dispense with those kinds of formalities, don't you? After all, we know each other so well now, don't we? At least, I know you well. Your sister Laura told me all about you when we met in the summer. You have a sweetheart who's a nurse and a lovely little niece and nephew, a handsome lad with blonde hair. I stumbled upon you on the day of the Hospital Carnival and watched you all together for some time. Then Laura told me all about your work moving furniture. That's how I finally tracked you down. Of course, all that was some time ago, but as they say, revenge is a dish best served cold.'

'Revenge for what? As I remember, you picked a fight with me. If you got more than you bargained for it was no more than you deserved. If you didn't want a good hiding, why did you go into a docker's pub with your fascist mates and start spouting all that rubbish? What did you think you were going to achieve?'

If Fielding knew about Laura, the children and Winnie, he had to get away. Who knew what this lunatic might do otherwise?

As soon as he realised they were going to tie him to the chair, he'd tensed all his muscles and expanded his chest, in the hope the rope would be loose enough for him to escape. Now he wiggled his hands behind his back, but it was useless. He was no Houdini, and he couldn't get them free. They hadn't tied his feet, though. Maybe if he could get this Fielding chap closer . . .

'The downfall of your pathetic little communist plot for revolution, of course.' Fielding smiled, but there was no mirth in his eyes. 'The British Fascists were never going to sit by and let you Bolsheviks destroy democracy. There were groups like mine all over the country provoking violence from you brainless thugs. We wanted to make sure Mr Baldwin knew exactly what your game was.'

'It didn't work out so well for you, did it? Your fascist mates all ran away. You were the only one who got hurt and no one else even knew it had happened.'

Percy looked around the room. There was a thin chink of light around one edge of the door. It didn't look as if it was completely shut. Were monkey man and his mates waiting outside? If he could somehow get Fielding closer, he might be able to use his legs to catch him off balance and make him drop the gun. He might then be able to move himself and the chair. He slowly shifted his weight forward and felt the back legs of the chair rise. It was unlikely to work, but it was the only thing he could come up with.

'Granted, my associates lost their nerve on that occasion. I may have made an error of judgement in choosing you and your thuggish friends as targets. On the whole, though, our plan worked perfectly. We provoked violence and riots all over England, ensuring Mr Baldwin realised the threat of revolution was real. Once the TUC understood that the strike had been infiltrated by Bolsheviks, it was only a matter of time until they got scared and conceded defeat.'

'It didn't work so well for you on Southampton Common, though, did it? Your fascist group may have been successful, but your own little mob made no difference at all. There were no riots here, no violence. In fact, I was the one who made sure of that at the dock gate.'

Percy looked towards the door again. Maybe it was wishful thinking, but he could swear the chink of light had grown bigger. He wriggled his hands some more. Was the rope getting looser? If he could just buy a little more time, he might be able to get his hands free. Gun or no gun, Fielding was no match for him if he could get untied.

'We may have lost the battle, Percy, but we won the war. The strike was broken because of our intervention, and the Bolshevik plot for revolution came to nothing.'

'But the coal miners are still out on strike, even though their children are starving. They haven't given in, so you haven't won yet.'

Percy wiggled his hands some more. The rope was definitely looser. He looked towards the door again. Lenny would be waiting for him in the Bristol Hotel. How he wished he was with him now, a pint in front of him. Was that chink of light really growing, or was he imagining it?

'But we will, Percy. It's only a matter of time. The Bolsheviks will never win here in England. Churchill called them, "Ferocious baboons capering amid the ruins of cities and the corpses of their victims," and he wasn't far wrong.'

'They showed how powerful working-class men like me are, though, didn't they? You can beat some of us down, starve us, shoot us even—' he looked pointedly at the gun '—but you can't kill all of us, and the more you try to keep us down, the more we're likely to revolt.'

'Oh, Percy, are you still clinging so tightly to your ideas of a revolution? The communists may have had their way in Russia, they may have even defeated and murdered my men fighting with the

White Russians in Murmansk, but they will never win here in England.'

'And you fascists will?'

'I believe we will. We are willing to do whatever it takes to protect the British state against socialist parasites and revolutionary reds like you plotting to bring down our king and our empire.'

'Even murder?'

'This is war, Percy. There is no such thing as murder in war.'

'Except when it comes to your men in Murmansk?'

'You and your kind aren't even fit to lick the boots of those men.' Fielding spat out the words and waved the gun wildly.

Percy had obviously hit a nerve, but in doing so, he might have overplayed his hand.

53 - Saturday 18 September 1926

The Bristol Hotel was still fairly empty. A couple of men in flat caps were leaning on the bar and another couple were seated at a table towards the back of the pub. It was an unremarkable place, square and ugly on the outside and sparsely furnished on the inside. Lenny had been in here once or twice with Percy, but he wasn't exactly fond of it.

'Ain't you Percy Barfoot's brother?' Apart from his rather unruly grey hair, the landlord was as unremarkable as his pub. Every landlord of every pub in the town knew Percy, though.

'Yes, he'll be along in a while.' Lenny put his coins onto the scratched mahogany bar and picked up his drink. 'He's got some business in the furniture restorers across the road.'

'Furniture restorers?' The landlord wrinkled his brow.

'Yes, across the road in the arches.'

'Must be new. They seem to change hands every five minutes. I've seen some toffs going in and out of there recently. They ain't been in here, though, and I ain't seen no furniture neither.'

Lenny found a seat by the window with a good view of the door he'd seen Percy go through. He sipped his drink and gazed listlessly across the street. He walked past these doorways under the road every day and always thought of them as arches. Now, as he sat staring at them, he saw they were squarer than he'd imagined. The sides were straight, with a gentle arch of terracotta brick at the top. If the furniture place really had just opened, perhaps Percy wouldn't be long.

The sips of beer did little to assuage his growing hunger. Hopefully, Laura had cooked something substantial because he could eat a horse. Being pregnant suited her. She had a wonderful pink-gold glow about her, like the light at dawn. He was so proud of her, and the little bump at her belly that grew bigger every day. If this new house was as good as Percy seemed to think it was, he might finally be able to get her and the children away from the coal dust in the air and the mould on the walls, just as they deserved.

A movement across the street caught his attention. Three men had come out of the door under the road. He took a swig of his drink and made ready to leave the pub. Then, with a tingle of anxiety, he realised none of the men was Percy. They were bunched together chatting. He narrowed his eyes and watched them walking towards the docks. Where was Percy? Then, with a stab of horror, he recognised the monkey-faced man he'd seen on the common with the fascist who'd caused Percy all that trouble back in May. Something was badly wrong.

Leaving his beer on the table, Lenny dashed to the door. He looked down the road. The men had disappeared. Either they'd been running, or they'd turned up Bridge Road or Oxford Street. In three strides he was outside the archway door. His heart was hammering in his ears and his stomach was churning, but he knew charging inside would be a mistake. He could hear voices, but not what they were saying. One of the voices was Percy's. He put his hand on the handle of the door and slowly began to ease it open, worried the hinges would creak. They didn't. He was almost afraid to breathe.

When the door was open a few inches, he peered inside. It was like a crypt, dimly lit and damp smelling. In the gloom, he could just make out the shape of a man in a dark suit with his back to the door. Behind him, he could see the good side of Percy's face, his shoulder and his arm. He was seated, and his expression said not by choice. With a long, slow breath, Lenny inched the door further, just enough to squeeze his thin body inside. Something about the scene in front of him stank of trouble. He had no idea what he was going to do about it, but he had to do something.

It was so dark he didn't see the steps. Thankfully, the man was talking about White Russians and men being murdered in Murmansk, so he didn't hear the slight gasp as Lenny missed his footing and caught himself. He took a slow, careful step closer. He could see Percy better now. It looked as if he was tied to the chair with his hands behind his back. Then he saw a glint of something metallic in the man's hand. He had a gun, and it was pointed at Percy.

Briefly, he thought about running back to the pub and asking the landlord to call the police, but what if they were too late? By the look in his eyes, he was sure Percy had seen him, although his face was perfectly still and calm. He shut his eyes very slowly then opened them again and looked hard at the gun, as if to make sure Lenny had seen it. Lenny nodded.

'So, you've won.' Percy looked at his feet, a picture of defeat. Lenny took another cautious step forward. With the advantage of his height, he could now see over the man's shoulder. He followed Percy's gaze and saw that his feet were unbound. 'You're going to kill me and get your revenge. No one knows I'm here, so I suppose you'll get away with it. Though surely even a condemned man deserves a last request?'

'It depends on what that request is,' the man said.

'Nothing difficult, just a last cigarette. I think it's traditional to allow at least that much? There's a packet in my jacket pocket and a box of matches.' Percy nodded towards his left jacket pocket.

'I suppose you think I'm going to untie your hands so you can smoke it?' the man laughed. 'Do you really think I'm that stupid?'

'No, but you could hold it for me. If you're really an officer and a man of honour like you say you are, you wouldn't deny me that much.'

The man paused. He seemed to be thinking. Lenny crept a little closer. He was almost in striking distance now and holding his breath in case he gave himself away.

When the man stepped toward Percy, Lenny couldn't tell if

he was going to get the cigarettes from his pocket or shoot him in the head. There was no time to dither. He leapt forward, grabbed his gun arm at the wrist and jerked it downwards. At the same moment, Percy kicked out with his legs. Their combined efforts and the element of surprise sent the man sprawling to the floor along with Lenny and Percy, who had somehow managed to tip the chair over while kicking out with his legs and yelling at the top of his voice.

A flash and a loud explosion filled the room. It rumbled around the curved walls. After that, everything was a chaotic blur; a tangle of arms, legs, chair and gun all struggling for supremacy. Despite all the flying punches and kicks raining down on him, and another loud, reverberating bang as the gun went off for a second time, Lenny held onto the man's wrist, slamming it onto the stone floor several times. With one last, hard thwack of the man's wrist against the floor, the gun skittered away.

Percy was still kicking and screaming. The man lunged desperately towards the weapon, but Lenny, by luck and his long arms more than judgement, managed to reach it first.

The man, on his knees now, froze as Lenny stood and pointed the barrel at his head. 'One move and I swear I'll shoot you,' he screamed.

The man sat back on his heels and put his hands on his head.

Percy was still on the floor wrestling with the chair. He'd managed to get his hands free, but the rope was still wound around his chest. Without taking his eyes off the man, Lenny went down on one knee and tried to help. His hands were trembling as he struggled with the knots holding Percy to the chair. With one hand holding the gun and his eyes firmly on the man, it was an impossible task. He reached into his pocket with his free hand, pulled out the penknife he used to sharpen his pencils at work and passed it to Percy to cut himself free.

When he stood up again, he began to feel very strange. Percy had freed himself from the chair and struggled to his knees. Lenny's head was spinning. Was he having a heart attack? Percy was speaking, but he couldn't hear him. Why was Percy staring at his gut like that? He looked down, following the line of Percy's horrified eyes. A dark stain was spreading across his white shirt on his right side, just above the waistband of his trousers. As he fell to his knees, Percy took the gun from his hands. There was another loud, echoing bang and flash, and then everything went black.

54 - Sunday 19 September 1926

Lenny's face was so pale it was almost the same colour as the pillow beneath his head. His skin, like vellum stretched thinly over his skull, showed every contour of bone, every vein. Laura moved her eyes from his face to his chest. She held her breath until she saw an almost imperceptible movement under the thin grey blanket and then exhaled in a long, slow sigh. Finally, she reached out and touched the hand resting on his chest. She wanted to check it was still warm. It was a ritual she'd performed many times since Winnie brought her a chair to sit beside his bed. They'd tried to make her go home to sleep, but she couldn't leave him in case he knew and thought she was letting him go. Winnie said the danger had passed and he was only sleeping, but he looked so much like a corpse she had to keep reassuring herself he was alive.

She closed her eyes and put her hand to her swelling belly with another slow sigh. She tried to envision the baby growing inside her but all she saw was Charlie's face, as he stood at her door with a look so grim she knew someone had died.

'There's been an accident,' he'd said.

She'd thought it must be that blasted motor lorry. Lenny and Percy said they were safe, but she didn't like them. They went too fast, made too much noise and created such a stench. She couldn't see what was wrong with a horse and cart, like the milkman, the baker and the coal man used. At least the waste that came out of a horse had some use. Percy had given Charlie money for the taxicab, or so he said. He didn't want her to walk, and he didn't want her to worry. How could she not worry?

It all ran through her head like something at the picture house. Percy and Winnie waiting for her at the hospital. Winnie saying she'd spoken to the sister on the ward and told her Lenny was her brother-in-law, so she'd better take good care of him. Lenny was lucky, she said. The bullet hadn't hit any vital organs and he would be fine. Laura couldn't see how being shot was lucky, or how it was an accident, either. Bullets didn't just accidentally fire out of guns. What were they even doing with a gun in the first place? Why did everything have to turn into such a drama whenever Percy was involved? Then he told her about Edgar Fielding, and she realised she'd played a part in it herself with her big mouth and her habit of talking to strangers.

'You couldn't have known,' Percy said, but she felt she should have all the same. When she asked why Lenny was even there, he told her about the house with the privy near the door. She understood she was responsible for that, too.

'If he hadn't been there,' Percy said, 'I'd have been the one that got shot, and it wouldn't have been a flesh wound, it'd have been a bullet through my head.'

'No chance of hitting any vital organs there.' It was a cruel thing to say, but she was angry with him. If he hadn't had that fight in the Bell and Crown, none of this would have happened.

Then Winnie said they were looking for people to donate for a transfusion because Lenny had lost so much blood. 'He can have some of mine,' said Percy. 'It's the same as his. He gave me his blood after I was blown up.'

She hadn't known that. Neither of them had ever told her. They didn't speak about France or what happened there much, at least not in front of her.

Laura opened her eyes again and looked at Lenny's sleeping face. Then she moved her eyes to his chest and held her breath, before exhaling with a sigh as she saw him inhale. She reached out and touched his hand to feel the warmth of his skin, and he curled his fingers around hers. She looked at his face again and his pale lashes fluttered. Then his eyes opened, and he smiled. She'd thought she'd never see those steel-blue eyes again, or that grin. She began to cry.

'Is Percy all right?' He turned his head towards her.

'He's fine. Not a single mark on him.' She brought his hand to her lips and kissed his fingers.

'Typical bloody Percy. He starts a war and walks away unscathed. Am I going to be all right?'

'Winnie says so. You were lucky, it was just a flesh wound,

but you lost a lot of blood. Percy gave you some of his. It's a good job we paid our thruppence a week into that hospital scheme. If we hadn't, I'd have had to start pawning things to pay for all this.'

'At least we'll get our money's worth.' He squeezed her hand again. 'What about the fascist chap? Did they get him?'

'Fielding? Yes, he's been arrested, but he's here in the hospital somewhere because of his wounds. He's under police guard, though.'

'What wounds?' Lenny frowned.

'Percy shot him. He told Charlie you passed out and dropped the gun. He said Fielding went for it, there was a struggle and Percy shot him.'

'Oh.' Lenny closed his eyes again and was silent for a long time. Then he added, 'I remember hearing another shot. That must have been what happened.'

55 - Sunday 19 September 1926

Lenny stared at the stark white ceiling. The disinfectant smell reminded him of being in hospital after he was gassed. The side of his belly hurt. The morphine they'd given him was wearing off, but the burning, throbbing pain was better than a fuzzy brain, so long as he didn't try to move. Laura had gone home, and he was on his own. When Winnie came to check on him and found her sound asleep in the chair still holding his hand, she'd woken her, given her some money for a taxicab and ordered her to go home. Laura tried to protest but Winnie insisted. She was a brave woman to stand up to Laura, he had to give her that much.

Lenny wished he could have gone with her, but Winnie said he'd have to stay in the hospital for a few more days to make sure he didn't get an infection. Percy would be back later, she said. He'd gone to his mother's house to see the children and then to Frank's to let him know what had happened. She said a reporter from the *Echo* had been sniffing around asking the police lots of questions, but she'd told them he was too sick to talk to them. Apparently, Edgar Fielding was a decorated officer. He'd won a DSO in Murmansk. He was a war hero, but the press was fond of tearing down heroes, especially fascist ones, and there were hints he had a history of mental instability.

Lenny thought he should probably ask someone to send a

telegram to his mother. He didn't expect her to come all the way from Alton to see him, but he didn't want her to find out by reading the newspaper. His family, or what was left of it, were dispersed all over the country. Bea was in Bristol with her husband, Eva was in Romsey working in a big house and Harry was likely at sea. None of them were going to come to see him. He didn't mind. Laura, the children and Percy were all the family he needed. For all their bickering and dramas, he loved them dearly and wouldn't swap them for anything. He smiled and closed his eyes.

*

He must have fallen asleep, because when he opened his eyes again, Percy was in the chair beside his bed. Apart from the shadow of stubble on his chin, he looked as fresh as a daisy, with no hint in his face or bearing of the horrors of the day before.

'You know you snore like a bloody freight train going up a hill?' Percy grinned at him. 'I don't know how Laura puts up with you.'

'I think she tolerates me because I keep saving her bloody brother's skin,' he replied with a smile. 'Although I'm still not sure how we got out of that place alive, or how you managed to get in that predicament in the first place.'

He closed his eyes again as Percy explained how Fielding's men had been following him around for months trying to find out where he lived, and how Laura had inadvertently helped them find him.

'I had it all under control before you turned up, you know.'

'Really?' Lenny opened his eyes again. 'It didn't look like it from where I was standing.'

'I was just keeping the bugger talking while I got my hands untied. When they tied me up, I did the old Houdini escape trick Wally taught us in France. The idiots left my legs untied, so I knew if I could get him close enough, I could knock him over and either get the gun away from him or get him to fire it without actually hitting me. Once he fired the gun, I was fairly sure someone would hear it and come to investigate. It was bound to make a lot of noise in that place.'

'That's a whole lot of probables and maybes.' Lenny raised his eyebrows. 'What if it hadn't worked?'

'Well, the people coming to investigate part certainly worked. Apparently the landlord of The Bristol saw you dash out like a scalded cat and, when he heard the gun go off, he came running across the road.'

'So, what you're saying is that I needn't have bothered rescuing you at all?'

'I hadn't bargained on you getting involved, but I've never been so happy to see you in my life. There was no guarantee my plan was going to work, and if it didn't . . .' Percy stopped smiling.

Now Lenny could see the strain in his face. He might be laughing and joking and trying to make light of it, but underneath his bravado he was struggling to hold it together.

'Happy birthday by the way.' Lenny tried to lift the mood. The last thing he needed was for Percy to go into one of his melancholies. 'I was going to take you out for a drink, but I think I'll have to give it a miss tonight.'

'I'm surprised you even remembered, but I'll let you off, seeing as I might not have lived to see thirty if it wasn't for you.'

'Well, if you could just manage to spend the next thirty years being boring and ordinary and not getting into any trouble, I might still buy you a drink when I get out of here. I'm not sure my poor old heart can cope with another thirty odd years of this kind of drama.'

'I'll try, but you know me, I can't promise anything.' Percy winked.

That was when Lenny discovered how much it hurt to laugh. There was a long silence while he tried to get the red, hot pain under control. Percy watched with a distressed look on his face. 'Do you want me to get a nurse to give you some morphine or something?'

'No, I need to keep my wits about me.' Lenny gritted his

teeth and tried to keep perfectly still. 'Winnie said there were reporters about asking questions, and I think the police will be coming to speak to me later.'

'You don't need to worry about that kind of thing. Winnie has told the sister on this ward to keep the reporters away from you, and I've already told the police everything.'

'Everything?' Lenny looked sideways at him. 'Including how Fielding came to be shot? Only I have to admit, I'm a bit hazy on that myself.'

The last thing he remembered before passing out was Percy taking the gun off him and Fielding kneeling with his hands on his head.

'Officially, you dropped the gun. There was a scuffle between me and Fielding and somehow he got shot.' Percy rubbed his chin and looked sheepish.

'And unofficially?'

'When I realised he'd shot you, I shot the bugger in the thigh. I'd have aimed for his head if I'd thought I could get away with it. He's a bloody lunatic.' Percy puffed out his cheeks and ran his hand through his hair. 'Charlie says he was in the asylum for over a year after he got back from Russia in nineteen-nineteen. Shell shock, apparently. He lost all his men in Murmansk, fighting with the White Russians against the Bolsheviks, and it sent him mad. When I heard that, I almost felt bad about shooting him.'

'Is he going to be all right?'

'Eventually, but it'll take him a lot longer to recover than it'll take you, and even then, he'll likely be in gaol, or the asylum again for trying to kill us.'

'So, we don't have to worry about him coming back to finish us off?'

'No. I think he's learned his lesson. You know, he told me I'd made a mistake hitting him. Perhaps I did, but I think he's beginning to realise he made a bigger mistake messing with me.' Percy was grinning again now.

'Laura said you'd given me some of your blood? Is that true?'

'Yes.' Percy pulled at his ear and looked uncomfortable. 'I suppose you could call it paying you back for the blood you gave me in France.'

'So, you were giving me my own blood back, then? Are you that determined to keep me in your debt?' Lenny laughed again and then winced at the pain.

'You never owed me anything in the first place, Len.' Percy shook his head sadly.

'You mean I've spent the last ten years trying to pay you back for nothing?'

'Listen, Len, I know you think you were somehow responsible for me getting blown up, and you have some debt to repay for that, and for me looking after you when you first arrived in France, but, frankly, that's a load of bollocks. It wasn't your fault I got blown up. I was the one acting like I knew it all, and when I saw Billy Simms lying there rotting, I stopped paying attention when I should have been keeping my head down. As for looking after you in the beginning, don't you think Wally and Joe and Corporal Brodrick did the same for me when I arrived? Didn't you look after the younger ones yourself, later on? Did you expect them to be indebted to you forever? Of course you didn't, you silly bugger. Anyway, if you want to play that game, then from now on, it must be time for me to look after you.'

Lenny closed his eyes again. Maybe, just maybe, Percy was right. He had helped plenty of young recruits over in France. He'd done it because he knew exactly how they were feeling, and because helping them not to be scared stopped him thinking about how scared he was himself. Not once had he expected anything in return, so why had he thought he owed Percy anything? If what Percy said was true, and it really wasn't his fault that he'd got blown up, then he really didn't owe him anything at all. For the first time in ten years, he felt free of the burden of guilt and obligation. It was a strange feeling, but he thought he might be able to get used to it.

56 - Saturday 29 January 1927

Winnie looked like a beautiful sprite in the white satin drop waist dress. The scalloped hem revealed the layer of lace beneath. It matched the lace of her veil, just as the crown of pale blue flowers matched her eyes. Percy took her hand. He could hardly believe she was his wife now. When Frank shut the door of Bert's car, Percy tore his eyes from Winnie to look through the window at the little group standing outside the Bell and Crown.

Winnie's parents were arm in arm a little way from everyone else. They looked faintly uncomfortable. It wasn't the nicest pub for a wedding reception, but it was the only place he'd have ever wanted one. Amy Medway waved her brawny arms wildly, even though they hadn't started moving yet. Mum wiped a tear from her eye and Dad put his arm around her shoulder. They were probably tears of relief at finally being shot of him. Behind them, Lizzie and Jim, Willy and Bea and Ethel and Ernie were chatting and paying no attention to the car. Maria stood beside them, but not really with them, with her hands on Stanley's shoulders. She was looking towards the car but not at him or Winnie. Her attention was focused on Frank getting into the driver's seat, he was sure of it. They'd been getting cosy together all day, and it was clear there was an attraction between them. Perhaps there'd be another wedding soon.

Then there was Laura, with little baby Ronald in her arms

wrapped in a shawl against the cold. Lenny had his arm around the pair of them and a silly, soppy look on his face. Since he'd been working for Frank, he'd put on weight, or maybe muscle. It suited him, made him look less lanky. A man that tall needed a bit of weight to him. Laura was fussing with the baby. Her hair had fallen across her face and the sun caught the copper highlights in its waves. Ronald was only five days old, so it had been touch and go whether she'd make it to the wedding, but she'd said wild horses wouldn't keep her away. He owed her and Lenny more than he could ever repay.

He thought about the table in Bert's workshop. They'd got it from the lady in the big house in Bassett. She'd said they could have it for firewood because it was so scuffed and bashed up, she didn't want it in her new house. Bert had rubbed it all down for him and was painting it with layers of yacht varnish. It might be second hand, but there was no shame in that. Rich people's cast offs were better than anything new he could afford. Frank, with the help of Bert, was thinking about branching out into furniture restoration. There was a certain irony in that after what had happened with Edgar Fielding.

The table was a gift for Laura. It was her birthday next week, and he couldn't wait to see her face when she saw it. When they'd moved her few bits of furniture to the new house, the old kitchen table had barely made it in one piece. The wonky legs were now even wonkier and, if you weren't careful, when you leaned on it all your tea ended up in the saucer. She deserved nice things, just like she deserved the new house away from the gasworks and the railway line. Compared to some of the fancy houses they worked in, the little terraces weren't the nicest, but they did have privies right by the back door and the street was quiet. Of course, he wouldn't be living there anymore now. He'd be living with Winnie and her parents. It would be a huge change, but her father, Bill, was at sea most of the time, and her mother, Amelia, seemed to like him.

The car began to move away. They could have walked to the Dolphin Hotel, but Bert insisted on lending them the car and Frank insisted on driving. There was a metallic clatter from the rear and Percy laughed as he saw Gladys and Bobby running away giggling. 'Those little buggers have tied tin cans to the car.' He turned to Winnie with a smile.

'It's traditional.' She smiled back. 'It'll bring us good luck.'

He looked into her eyes, the same colour as the sky they'd been lucky enough to have for their wedding day. He must already be the luckiest man in the world.

Acknowledgements

This book is a work of fiction inspired by my maternal grandparents Leonard and Laura White. Sadly, I never met Leonard, but he appeared in my first book, *Plagued*, as Lofty, one of the men fighting in France with Thomas. The real Leonard White joined the Devonshire Regiment in 1914, aged sixteen, and was later transferred to the Hampshire Regiment but served in Gallipoli, Egypt and Palestine, not France. Leonard was the second of Harry and Ada White's six children. They lived in Standford Street, Northam. Harry was a porter in the docks' stores. After the war, Leonard followed in his father's footsteps and became a warehouse porter. As there are no family photos of Leonard, I had to imagine him. I gave him blonde hair, like his eldest son, Robert. The blonde streak running through my family had to come from somewhere, after all. I also made him tall, another trait that runs through my family, although it bypassed me.

Laura was the youngest of six children born to Frank and Emma Hebditch of Kent Road, St Denys. She died when I was just four, but I remember her tin of sweets and the fairy tales she told me. She was larger than life, always laughing, and fond of a bottle of stout and a cigarette. In later life she lived in Carnation Road, where the locals all knew her, and her door was always open to her friends and family.

Percy also appeared in *Plagued*. He was loosely based on Laura's older brother, Percy Hebditch. The real Percy joined the territorial force before the war, aged 17, and was later in the Hampshire Regiment in India. He was discharged from the army in March 1917. His Silver War Badge records mention, amongst other things, delusional insanity, a condition that would later be recognised as shell shock, or PTSD. Like his sister, I imagine he was quite a character, although perhaps not quite like the one in my story.

Southampton's part in the General Strike of 1926 was brought to life by Will Boisseau's informative article in the Southampton Local History Forum Journal, and the TUC library, where I found copies of Southampton Strike Bulletins. Adrian Weir's newsletter in the History Group of the Communist Party of Britain was also thought provoking. It gave an alternative slant on Boisseau's story of men who 'lost their lives or their limbs in the docks as unqualified men tried to work heavy machinery.' Weir's version had them as 'Two dockers killed due to management scabbing and trying to operate cranes.' The truth is probably somewhere between the two.

General information about the strike came from the National Archives and SparticusEducational.com. The Old Bailey Online and the National Archives gave an insight into trial procedures and the workings of the Winchester Assizes. History.com had useful facts about the use of fingerprint evidence and the 1905 trail of the Stratton Brothers. HistoryExtra.com helped with my understanding of the Russian Civil War and the British campaign against the Bolsheviks.

Fate also played a part. Laura and Leonard White lived on Melbourne Street, but the houses were either flattened by the Luftwaffe, or demolished as part of the 1960's slum clearance. In response to a plea on several local history Facebook groups for information about the area I had a message from a lovely gentleman called Roger Stevens. After the Second World War, his family lived in the house my grandparents once rented, and his memories were more helpful than I can say. They also confirmed the poverty and depravation my mother recalled.

Once again, Danielle Wrate, of Wrate's Editing Services, and proofreader Abby Sparks, gave me the advice and encouragement I needed to bring this story to print and Aleks Kruz, and Hayley Yates of Hangar47, provided the technical expertise. Last, but definitely not least, I have to thank my long-suffering husband, Dave Keates, for his patience in listening to the story, believing in me, and giving his feedback.

This book may owe a lot to Laura, Leonard and Percy but it is really a story about the lasting brotherhood between the men who came back from the Great War, and the struggles faced by the working-class people of Northam between the wars. It is a tribute to their spirit, and the tight knit community they built, even though they never saw the land fit for heroes they were promised.

ABOUT THE AUTHOR

Marie Keates is a writer, blogger and walker, who can't resist the mystery of an unexplored trail and is mad about history. She lives in Southampton, and has spent much of her life working in the travel industry and writing copy on such diverse subjects as travel, canals, running and coffee. Her interest in Southampton's history has made her blog, www.iwalkalone.co.uk popular with local history groups, ex Sotonians and visitors to the city. Her debut novel, *Plagued*, was inspired by research into her family history and stories she heard at her grandfather's knee.

Printed in Great Britain
by Amazon

82011646R00159